Robert Williams Buchanan

Saint Abe and His Seven Wives

A tale of Salt Lake City with a bibliographical note

Robert Williams Buchanan

Saint Abe and His Seven Wives
A tale of Salt Lake City with a bibliographical note

ISBN/EAN: 9783337174033

Printed in Europe, USA, Canada, Australia, Japan

Cover: Foto ©Andreas Hilbeck / pixelio.de

More available books at **www.hansebooks.com**

SAINT ABE AND HIS SEVEN WIVES

A Tale of Salt Lake City

WITH A BIBLIOGRAPHICAL NOTE

BY

ROBERT BUCHANAN

FIRST CHEAP EDITION

LONDON

ROBERT BUCHANAN

36, GERRARD STREET, SHAFTESBURY AVENUE, W.

1896

CONTENTS.

—◆—

TO OLD DAN CHAUCER.

Maypole dance and Whitsun ale,
Sports of peasants in the dale,
Harvest mirth and junketting,
Fireside play and kiss-in-ring,
Ancient fun and wit and ease,—
Gone are one and all of these;
All the pleasant pastime planned
In the green old Mother-land:
Gone are these and gone the time
Of the breezy English rhyme,
Sung to make men glad and wise
By great Bards with twinkling eyes:
Gone the tale and gone the song
Sound as nut-brown ale and strong,
Freshening the sultry sense
Out of idle impotence,

Sowing features dull or bright
With deep dimples of delight!

Thro' the Mother-land I went,
Seeking these, half indolent :
Up and down, I saw them not :
Only found them, half-forgot,
Buried in long-darken'd nooks
With thy barrels of old books,
Where the light and love and mirth
Of the morning days of earth
Sleeps, like light of sunken suns
Brooding deep in cob-webb'd tuns !
Everywhere I found instead,
Hanging her dejected head,
Barbing shafts of bitter wit,
The pale Modern Spirit sit—.
While her shadow, great as Gog's,
Cast upon the island fogs,
In the midst of all things dim
Loom'd, gigantically grim.

Honest Chaucer, thee I greet
In a verse with blithesome feet,
And tho' modern bards may stare,
Crack a passing joke with Care !
Take a merry song and true
Fraught with inner meanings too !
Goodman Dull may croak and scowl :—
Leave him hooting to the owl !
Tight-laced Prudery may turn
Angry back with eyes that burn,
Reading on from page to page
Scrofulous novels of the age !
Fools may frown and humbugs rail,
Not for them I tell the Tale ;
Not for them, but souls like thee,
Wise old English JOLLITY !

Newport, October, 1871.

ST. ABE AND HIS SEVEN WIVES.

Art thou unto a helpmate bound ?
  Then stick to her, my brother !
But hast thou laid her in the ground ?
  Don't go to seek another !
Thou hast not sin'd, if thou hast wed,
  Like many of our number,
But thou hast spread a thorny bed,
  And there alas ! must slumber !

ST. PAUL, COR. I., 7, 27-28.

O let thy fount of love be blest
  And let thy wife rejoice,
Contented rest upon her breast
  And listen to her voice ;
Yea, be not ravish'd from her side
  Whom thou at first has chosen,
Nor having tried one earthly bride
  Go sighing for a Dozen !

SOL. PROV. V., 18-20.

PASSING THE RANCHE.

"GRRR!" shrieked the boss, with teeth clench'd
    tight,
Just as the lone ranche hove in sight,
And with a face of ghastly hue
He flogg'd the horses till they flew,
As if the devil were at their back,
Along the wild and stony track.
From side to side the waggon swung,
While to the quaking seat I clung.
Dogs bark'd; on each side of the pass
The cattle grazing on the grass
Raised heads and stared; and with a cry
Out the men rush'd as we roll'd by.

"Grrr!" shriek'd the boss; and o'er and o'er
He flogg'd the foaming steeds and swore;
Harder and harder grew his face
As by the ranche we swept apace,
And faced the hill, and past the pond,
And gallop'd up the height beyond,
Nor tighten'd rein till field and farm
Were hidden by the mountain's arm
A mile behind; when, hot and spent,
The horses paused on the ascent,
And mopping from his brow the sweat,
The boy glanced round with teeth still set,
And panting, with his eyes on me,
Smil'd with a look of savage glee.

Joe Wilson is the boss's name,
A Western boy well known to fame.
He goes about the dangerous land
His life for ever in his hand;

Has lost three fingers in a fray,
Has scalp'd his Indian too they say;
Between the white man and the red
Four times he hath been left for dead;
Can drink, and swear, and laugh, and brawl,
And keeps his big heart thro' it all
Tender for babes and women.

                                        He
Turned, smiled, and nodded savagely;
Then, with a dark look in his eyes
In answer to my dumb surprise,
Pointed with jerk of the whip's heft
Back to the place that we had left,
And cried aloud,

                    " I guess you think
I'm mad, or vicious, or in drink.
But theer you're wrong.   I never pass
The ranche down theer and bit of grass,
I never pass 'em, night nor day,
But the fit takes me jest that way!

The hosses know as well as me
What's coming, miles afore we see
The dern'd old corner of a place,
And they git ready for the race !
Lord ! if I *didn't* lash and sweer,
And ease my rage out passing theer,
Guess I should go clean mad, that's all.
And thet's the reason why I call
This turn of road where I am took
Jest Old Nick's Gallop !"

                        Then his look
Grew more subdued yet darker still ;
And as the horses up the hill
With loosen'd rein toil'd slowly, he
Went on in half soliloquy,
Indifferent almost if I heard,
And grimly grinding out each word.

II

JOE WILSON GOES A-COURTING.

"There was a time, and no mistake,
When thet same ranche down in the brake
Was pleasanter a heap to me
Than any sight on land or sea.
The hosses knew it like their master,
Smelt it miles orf, and spank'd the faster!
Ay, bent to reach thet very spot,
Flew till they halted steaming hot
Sharp opposite the door, among
The chicks and children old and young ;
And down I'd jump, and all the go
Was 'Fortune, boss!' and 'Welcome, Joe!'
And Cissy with her shining face,
Tho' she was missus of the place,

Stood larfing, hands upon her hips ;
And when upon her rosy lips
I put my mouth and gave her one,
She'd cuff me, and enjy the fun !
She was a widow young and tight,
Her chap had died in a free fight,
And here she lived, and round her had
Two chicks, three brothers, and her dad,
All making money fast as hay,
And doing better every day.
Waal ! guess tho' I was peart and swift,
Spooning was never much my gift ;
But Cissy was a gal so sweet,
So fresh, so spicy, and so neat,
It put your wits all out o' place,
Only to star' into her face.
Skin whiter than a new-laid egg,
Lips full of juice, and sech a leg !
A smell about her, morn and e'en,
Like fresh-bleach'd linen on a green ;

And from her hand when she took mine,
The warmth ran up like sherry wine;
And if in liquor I made free
To pull her larfing on my knee,
Why, there she'd sit, and feel so nice,
Her heer all scent, her breath all spice!
See! women hate, both young and old,
A chap that's over shy and cold,
And fire of all sorts kitches quick,
And Cissy seem'd to feel full slick
The same fond feelings, and at last
Grew kinder every time I passed;
And all her face, from eyes to chin,
Said 'Bravo, Joe! You're safe to win!'
And tho' we didn't fix, d'ye see,
In downright *words* that it should be,
Ciss and her fam'ly understood
That she and me would jine for good.
Guess I was like a thirsty hoss
Dead beat for days, who comes across

A fresh clear beck, and on the brink
Scoops out his shaky hand to drink;
Or like a gal or boy of three,
With eyes upon a pippin-tree;
Or like some Injin cuss who sees
A bottle ot rum among the trees,
And by the bit of smouldering log,
Where squatters camp'd and took their grog
The night afore.   Waal!" (here he ground
His teeth again with savage sound)
" Waal, stranger, fancy, jest for fun,
The feelings of the thirsty one,
If, jest as he scoop'd out his hand,
The water turn'd to dust and sand !
Or fancy how the lad would scream
To see thet fruit-tree jest a dream !
Or guess how thet poor Injin cuss,
Would dance and swear, and screech and fuss,
If when he'd drawn the cork and tried
To get a gulp of rum inside,

'Twarn't anything in thet theer style,
But physic stuff or stinking ile !
Ah ! you've a notion now, I guess,
Of how all ended in a mess,
And how when I was putting in
My biggest card and thought to win,
The Old One taught her how to cheat,
And yer I found myself, clean beat !'"

III

SAINT AND DISCIPLE.

Joe Wilson paused, and gazed straight down,
With gritting teeth and bitter frown,
And not till I entreated him
Did he continue,—fierce and grim,
With knitted brow and teeth clench'd tight.

" Along this way one summer night,
Jest as I meant to take the prize,
Passed an APOSTLE—dern his eyes !
On his old pony, gravel-eyed,
His legs a-dangling down each side,
With twinkling eyes and wheedling smile,
Grinning beneath his broad-brimm'd tile,

With heer all scent and shaven face,
He came a-trotting to the place.
My luck was bad, I wasn't near,
But busy many a mile from yer;
And what I tell was told to me
By them as were at hand to see.
'Twarn't every day, I reckon, they
Saw an Apostle pass their way!
And Cissy, being kind o' soft,
And empty in the upper loft,
Was full of downright joy and pride
To hev thet saint at her fireside—
One of the seventy they call
The holiest holy—dern 'em all!
O he was 'cute and no mistake,
Deep as Salt Lake, and wide awake!
Theer at the ranche three days he stayed,
And well he knew his lying trade.
'Twarn't long afore he heard full free
About her larks and thet with me,

And how 'twas quite the fam'ly plan
To hev me for her second man.
At fust thet old Apostle said
Little, but only shook his head ;
But you may bet he'd no intent
To let things go as things had went.
Three nights he stayed, and every night
He squeezed her hand a bit more tight ;
And every night he didn't miss
To give a loving kiss to Ciss ;
And tho' his fust was on her brow,
He ended with her mouth, somehow.
O, but he was a knowing one,
The Apostle Hiram Higginson !
Grey as a badger's was his heer,
His age was over sixty year
(Her grandfather was little older),
So short, his head just touch'd her shoulder;
His face all grease, his voice all puff,
His eyes two currants stuck in duff ;—

Call thet a man!—then look at *me*!
Thretty year old and six foot three,
Afear'd o' nothing morn nor night,
The man don't walk I wouldn't fight!
Women is women! Thet's their style—
Talk *reason* to them and they'll bile;
But baste 'em soft as any pigeon,
With lies and rubbish and religion;
Don't talk of flesh and blood and feeling,
But Holy Ghost and blessed healing;
Don't name things in too plain a way.
Look a heap warmer than you say,
Make 'em believe they're serving true
The Holy Spirit and not you,
Prove all the world but you's damnation,
And call your kisses jest salvation;
Do this, and press 'em on the sly,
You're safe to win 'em. Jest you try!

"Fust thing I heerd of all this game,
One night when to the ranche I came,

Jump'd down, ran in, saw Cissy theer,
And thought her kind o' cool and queer;
For when I caught her with a kiss,
'Twarn't that she took the thing amiss,
But kept stone cool and gev a sigh,
And wiped her mouth upon the sly
On her white milkin'-apron. 'Waal,'
Says I, 'you're out o' sorts, my gel!'
And with a squeamish smile for me,
Like folks hev when they're sick at sea,
Says she, 'O, Joseph, ere too late,
I am awaken'd to my state—
How pleasant and how sweet it is
To be in sech a state of bliss!'
I stared and gaped, and turned to Jim
Her brother, and cried out to him,
'Hullo, mate, what's the matter here?
What's come to Cissy? Is she *queer*?'
Jim gev a grin and answered ' Yes,
A trifle out o' sorts, I guess.'

But Cissy here spoke up and said,
'It ain't my stomach, nor my head,
It ain't my flesh, it ain't my skin,
It's holy *spirits* here within!'
'Waal,' says I, meanin' to be kind,
'I must be off, for I'm behind;
But next time that I pass this way
We'll fix ourselves without delay.
I know what your complaint is, Ciss,
I've seen the same in many a miss,
Keep up your spirits, thet's your plan,
You're lonely here without a man,
And you shall hev as good a one
As e'er druv hoss beneath the sun!'
At that I buss'd her with a smack,
Turn'd out, jump'd up, and took the track,
And larfing druv along the pass.

"Theer! Guess I was as green as grass!"

C

THE BOOK OF MORMON.

" 'Twas jest a week after thet day
When down I druv again this way.
My heart was light; and 'neath the box
I'd got a shawl and two fine frocks
For Cissy.   On in spanking style
The hosses went mile arter mile ;
The sun was blazing golden bright,
The sunflowers burning in the light,
The cattle in the golden gleer
Wading for coolness everywheer
Among the shinin' ponds, with flies
As thick as pepper round their eyes
And on their heads.   See! as I went
Whistling like mad and waal content,

Altho' 'twas broad bright day all round,
A cock crow'd, and I thought the sound
Seem'd pleasant.   Twice or thrice he
    crow'd,
And then up to the ranche I rode.
Since then I've often heerd folk say
When a cock crows in open day
It's a *bad sign*, announcin' clear
Black luck or death to those thet hear.

"When I drew up, all things were still.
I saw the boys far up the hill
Tossin' the hay ; but at the door
No Cissy stood as oft afore.
No, not a soul there, left nor right,
Her very chicks were out o' sight.
So down I jump'd, and 'Ciss !' I cried,
But not a sign of her outside.
With thet into the house I ran,
But found no sight of gel or man—

All empty.   Thinks I, ' this is queer ! '—
Look'd in the dairy—no one theer ;
Then loiter'd round the kitchen track
Into the orchard at the back :
Under the fruit-trees' shade I pass'd, . . .
Thro' the green bushes, . . . and at last
Found, as the furthest path I trode,
The gel I wanted.   Ye . . . s ! by —— !

" The gel I wanted—ay, I found
More than I wanted, you'll be bound !
Theer, seated on a wooden cheer,
With bows and ribbons in her heer,
Her hat a-swinging on a twig
Close by, sat Ciss in her best rig,
And at her feet that knowing one,
The Apostle Hiram Higginson !
They were too keen to notice me,
So I held back behind a tree

And watch'd 'em.   Never night nor day
Did I see Cissy look so gay,
Her eyes all sparkling blue and bright,
Her face all sanctified delight.
She hed her gown tuck'd up to show
Embrider'd petticoat below,
And jest a glimpse, below the white,
Of dainty leg in stocking tight
With crimson clocks; and on her knee
She held an open book, which he,
Thet dern'd Apostle at her feet,
With her low milking stool for seat,
Was reading out all clear and pat,
Keeping the place with finger fat;
Creeping more close to book and letter
To feel the warmth of his text better,
His crimson face like a cock's head
With his emotion as he read,
And now and then his eyes he'd close
Jest like a cock does when he crows!

Above the heads of thet strange twc
The shade was deep, the sky was blue,
The place was full of warmth and smell,
All round the fruit and fruit-leaves fell,
And that Saint's voice, when all was
    still,
Was like the groanin' of a mill.

"At last he stops for lack of wind,
And smiled with sarcy double-chinn'd
Fat face at Cissy, while she cried,
Rocking herself from side to side,
'O Bishop, them are words of bliss!'
And then he gev a long fat kiss
On her warm hand, and edged his stool
Still closer. Could a man keep cool
And see it? Trembling thro' and thro'
I walked right up to thet theer two,
And caught the dern'd old lump of duff
Jest by the breeches and the scruff.

And chuck'd him off, and with one kick
Sent his stool arter him right slick—
While Cissy scream'd with frighten'd face,
'Spare him! O spare that man of grace!'

"'Spare him!' I cried, and gev a shout,
'What's this yer shine you air about—
What cuss is this that I jest see
With that big book upon your knee,
Cuddling up close and making sham
To read a heap of holy flam?'
Then Cissy clasp'd her hands, and said,
While that dern'd Saint sat fierce and
        red,
Mopping his brow with a black frown,
And squatting where I chuck'd him down,
'Joe Wilson, stay your hand so bold,
Come not a wolf into the fold;
Forbear to touch that holy one—
The Apostle Hiram Higginson.'

'Touch him,' said I, 'for half a pin
I'd flay and quarter him and skin !
Waal may he look so white and skeer'd
For of his doings I have heerd ;
Five wives he hev already done,
And him—not half the man for one !'

"And then I stoop'd and took a peep
At what they'd studied at so deep,
And read, for I can read a bit,
'The Book of Mormon '—what was writ
By the first Saint of all the lot,
Mad Joseph, him the Yankees shot.
'What's the contents of this yer book ?'
Says I, and fixed her with a look.
'O Joe,' she answered, 'read aright,
It is a book of blessed light—
Thet holy man expounds it clear;
Edification great is theer !'

Then, for my blood was up, I took
One kick at thet infernal book,
And tho' the Apostle guv a cry,
Into the well I made it fly,
And turning to the Apostle cried,
 Tho' thet theer Scriptur' is your guide,
You'd best depart without delay,
Afore you sink in the same way!
And sure as fate you'll wet your skin
If you come courting yer agin!'

" At first he stared and puff'd and blew,—
'Git out!' I cried, and off he flew,
And not till he was out o' reach
Shook his fat fist and found his speech.
I turned to Cissy. 'Cicely Dunn,'
Ses I, ' is this a bit of fun
Or eernest?' Reckon 'twas a sight
To see the way she stood upright,

Rolled her blue eyes up, tried to speak,
Made fust a giggle, then a squeak,
And said half crying, 'I despise
Your wicked calumnies and lies,
And what you would insinuate
Won't move me from my blessed state.
Now I perceive in time, thank hiven,
You are a man to anger given,
Jealous and vi'lent. Go away!
And when you recollect this day,
And those bad words you've said to me,
Blush if you kin. Tehee! tehee!'
And then she sobbed, and in her cheer
Fell crying: so I felt quite queer,
And stood like a dern'd fool, and star'd
Watchin' the pump a going hard;
And then at last, I couldn't stand
The sight no more, but slipt my hand
Sharp into hers, and said quite kind,
'Say no more, Cissy—never mind;

I know how queer you women's ways is —
Let the Apostle go to blazes !'
Now thet was plain and fair.   With this
I would have put my arm round Ciss.
But Lord ! you should have seen her face,
When I attempted to embrace ;
Sprang to her feet and gev a cry,
Her back up like a cat's, her eye
All blazing, and cried fierce and clear,
'You villain, touch me if you deer !'
And jest then in the distance, fur
From danger, a voice echoed her,—
The dern'd Apostle's, from some place
Where he had hid his ugly face,—
Crying out faint and thick and clear,
'Yes, villain, touch her if you deer !'

So riled I was, to be so beat,
I could have struck her to my fect

I didn't tho', tho' sore beset—
I never struck a woman yet.

" But off I walked right up the pass,
And found the men among the grass,
And when I came in sight said flat,
' What's this yer game Cissy is at ?
She's thrown me off, and taken pity
On an Apostle from the City.
Five wives already, too, has he—
Poor cussed things as e'er I see—
Does she mean *mischief* or a *lark ?*'
Waal, all the men at thet look'd dark,
And scratch'd their heads and seem'd in
        doubt.
At last her brother Jim spoke out—
' Joe, don't blame *us*—by George, it's true,
We're chawed by this as much as you ;
We've done our best and tried and tried,
But Ciss is off her head with pride.

And all her thoughts, both night and day,
Are with the Apostles fur away.
" O that I were in bliss with them
Theer in the new Jerusalem!"
She says; and when we laugh and sneer,
Ses we're jest raging wolves down here.
She's a bit dull at home d'ye see,
Allays liked heaps of company,
And now the foolish critter paints
A life of larks among the Saints.
We've done our best, don't hev a doubt,
To keep the old Apostle out :
We've trained the dogs to seize and bite him,
We've got up ghosts at night to fright him,
Doctor'd his hoss and so upset him,
Put tickle-grass in bed to fret him,
Jalap'd his beer and snuffed his tea too,
Gunpowder in his pipe put free too;
A dozen times we've well-nigh kill'd him,
We've skeer'd him, shaken him, and spill'd
    him;

In fact, done all we deer,' said Jim,
'Against a powerful man like him ;
But all in vain we've hed our sport;
Jest like a cat that *can't* be hurt,
With nine good lives if he hev one,
Is this same Hiram Higginson !'"

JOE ENDS HIS STORY.—FIRST GLIMPSE OF UTAH.

Joe paused, for down the mountain's brow
His hastening horses trotted now.
Into a canyon green and light,
Thro' which a beck was sparkling light,
Quickly we wound.   Joe Wilson lit
His cutty pipe, and suck'd at it
In silence grim ; and when it drew,
Puff after puff of smoke he blew,
With blank eye fixed on vacancy.
At last he turned again to me,
And spoke with bitter indignation
The epilogue of his narration.

"Waal, stranger, guess my story's told,
The Apostle beat and I was bowl'd.

Reckon I might have won if I
Had allays been at hand to *try;*
But I was busy out of sight,
And he was theer, morn, noon, and night,
Playing his cards, and waal it weer
For him I never caught him theer.
To cut the story short, I guess
He got the Prophet to say ' yes,'
And Cissy without much ado
Gev her consent to hev him too ;
And one fine morning off they druv
To what he called the Abode of Love—
A dern'd old place, it seems to me,
Jest like a dove-box on a tree,
Where every lonesome woman-soul
Sits shivering in her own hole,
And on the outside, free to choose,
The old cock-pigeon struts and coos.
I've heard from many a one that Ciss
Has found her blunder out by this,

And she'd prefer for company
A brisk young chap, tho' poor, like me,
Than the sixth part of him she's won—
The holy Hiram Higginson.
I've got a peep at her since then,
When she's crawl'd out of thet theer den,
But she's so pale and thin and tame
I shouldn't know her for the same.
No flesh to pinch upon her cheek,
Her legs gone thin, no voice to speak,
Dabby and crush'd, and sad and flabby,
Sucking a wretched squeaking baby ;
And all the fun and all the light
Gone from her face, and left it white.
Her cheek 'll take a teeble flush,
But hesn't blood enough to blush ;
Tries to seem modest, peart and sly,
And brighten up if I go by,
But from the corner of her eyes
Peeps at me quietly, and sighs.

D

Reckon her luck has been a stinger!
She'd bolt if I held up my finger;
But tho' I'm rough, and wild, and free,
Take a *Saint's* leavings—no not me!
You've heerd of Vampires—them that rise
At dead o' night with flaming eyes,
And into women's beds 'll creep
To suck their blood when they're asleep.
I guess these Saints are jest the same,
Sucking the life out is their game;
And tho' it ain't in the broad sun
Or in the open streets it's done,
There ain't a woman they clap eyes on
Their teeth don't touch, their touch don't pison;
Thet's their dern'd way in this yer spot—
Grrr! git along, hoss! dern you, trot!"

From pool to pool the wild beck sped
Beside us, dwindled to a thread.

With mellow verdure fringed around
It sang along with summer sound :
Here gliding into a green glade ;
Here darting from a nest of shade
With sudden sparkle and quick cry,
As glad again to meet the sky ;
Here whirling off with eager will
And quickening tread to turn a mill ;
Then stealing from the busy place
With duskier depths and wearier pace
In the blue void above the beck
Sailed with us, dwindled to a speck,
The hen-hawk; and from pools below
The blue-wing'd heron oft rose slow,
And upward pass'd with measured beat
Of wing to seek some new retreat.
Blue was the heaven and darkly bright,
Suffused with throbbing golden light,
And in the burning Indian ray
A million insects hummed at play.

Soon, by the margin of the stream,
We passed a driver with his team
Bound for the City; then a hound
Afar off made a dreamy sound;
And suddenly the sultry track
Left the green canyon at our back,
And sweeping round a curve, behold!
We came into the yellow gold
Of perfect sunlight on the plain;
And Joe, abruptly drawing rein,
Said quick and sharp, shading his eyes
With sunburnt hand, "See, theer it
    lies—
Theer's *Sodom !*"

           And even as he cried,
The mighty Valley we espied,
Burning below us in one ray
Of liquid light that summer day;

And far away, 'mid peaceful gleams
Of flocks and herds and glistering streams,
Rose, fair as aught that fancy paints,
The wondrous City of the Saints!

THE CITY OF THE SAINTS.

O Saints that shine around the heavenly Seat !
What heaven is this that opens at my feet ?
What flocks are these that thro' the golden gleam
Stray on by freckled fields and shining stream ?
What glittering roofs and white kiosks are these,
Up-peeping from the shade of emerald trees ?
Whose City is this that rises on the sight
Fair and fantastic as a city of light
Seen in the sunset ?   What is yonder sea
Opening beyond the City cool and free,
Large, deep, and luminous, looming thro' the heat,
And lying at the darkly shadowed feet
Of the Sierras, which with jagged line
Burning to amber in the light divine,
Close in the Valley of the happy land,
With heights as barren as a dead man's hand?

O pilgrim, halt!   O wandering heart, give praise
Behold the City of these Latter Days!
Here may'st thou leave thy load and be forgiven,
And in anticipation taste of Heaven!

AMONG THE PASTURES.—SUMMER EVENING DIALOGUE.

BISHOP PETE. BISHOP JOSS. STRANGER.

BISHOP PETE.

AH, things down here, as you observe, are getting
more pernicious,

And Brigham's losing all his nerve, altho' the
fix is vicious.

Jest as we've rear'd a prosperous place and fill'd
our holy quivers,

The Yankee comes with dern'd long face to give
us all the shivers!

And on his jaws a wicked grin prognosticates
    disaster,
And, jest as sure as sin is sin, he means to be
    the master.
" Pack up your traps," I hear him cry, " for here
    there's no remainin',"
And winks with his malicious eye, and progues
    us out of Canaan.

BISHOP JOSS.

It ain't the Yankee that *I* fear, the neighbour
    nor the stranger—
No, no, it's closer home, it's *here*, that I perceive
    the danger.
The wheels of State has gather'd rust, the helm
    wants hands to guide it,
'Tain't from without the biler 'll bust, but 'cause
    of steam inside it ;
Yet if we went falootin' less, and made less
    noise and flurry,

It isn't Jonathan, I guess, would hurt us in a
hurry.

But there's sedition cast and west, and secret
revolution,

There's canker in the social breast, rot in the
constitution ;

And over half of us, at least, are plunged in mad
vexation,

Forgetting how our race increased, our very
creed's foundation.

What's our religion's strength and force, its
substance, and its story ?

STRANGER.

Polygamy, my friend, of course ! the law of love
and glory !

BISHOP PETE.

Stranger, I'm with you there, indeed :—it's been
the best of nusses ;

Polygamy is to our creed what meat and drink
  to *us* is.

Destroy that notion any day, and all the rest is
  brittle,

And Mormondom dies clean away like one in
  want of vittle.

It's meat and drink, it's life, it's power! to
  heaven its breath doth win us!

It warms our vitals every hour! it's Holy Ghost
  within us!

Jest lay that notion on the shelf, and all life's
  springs are frozen!

I've half-a-dozen wives myself, and wish I had a
  dozen!

Bishop Joss.

If all the Elders of the State like *you* were sound
  and holy,

P. Shufflebotham, guess our fate were far less
  melancholy.

You air a man of blessed toil, far-shining and
  discerning,

A heavenly lamp well trimm'd with oil, upon the
  altar burning.

And yet for every one of us with equal resolu-
  tion,

There's twenty samples of the Cuss, as mean as
  Brother Clewson.

STRANGER.

St. Abe?

BISHOP JOSS.

Yes, *him*—the snivelling sneak-—his very *name*
  provokes me,—

Altho' my temper's milky-meek, he sours me
  and he chokes me.

To see him going up and down with those meek
  lips asunder,

Jest like a man about to drown, with lead to sink
  him under,

His grey hair on his shoulders shed, one leg than
    t'other shorter,
No end of cuteness in his head, and him—as
    weak as water!

BISHOP PETE.

And yet how well I can recall the time when
    Abe was younger—
Why not a chap among us all went for the
    notion stronger.
When to the mother-country he was sent to wake
    the sinning,
He shipp'd young lambs across the sea by *flocks*
    —he was so winning;
O but he had a lively style, describing saintly
    blisses!
He made the spirit pant and smile, and seek
    seraphic kisses!
How the bright raptures of the Saint fresh lustre
    seemed to borrow,

While black and awful he did paint the one-wived
    sinner's sorrow!

Each woman longed to be his bride, and by his
    side to slumber—

" The more the blesseder!" he cried, still adding
    to the number.

STRANGER.

How did the gentleman contrive to change his
    skin so quickly ?

BISHOP JOSS.

The holy Spirit couldn't thrive because the Flesh
    was sickly!

Tho' day by day he did increase his flock, his
    soul was shallow,

His brains were only candle-grease, and wasted
    down like tallow.

He stoop'd a mighty heap too much, and let his
    household rule him,

The weakness of the man was such that any face
    could fool him.

Ay ! made his presence cheap, no doubt, and so
    contempt grew quicker,—

Not measuring his notice out in smallish drams,
    like liquor.

His house became a troublous house, with mis-
    chief overbrimmin',

And he went creeping like a mouse among the
    cats of women.

Ah, womenfolk are hard to rule, their tricks is
    most surprising,

It's only a dern'd spoony fool goes *sentimental-
    ising!*

But give 'em now and then a bit of notice and a
    present,

And lor, they're just like doves, that sit on one
    green branch, all pleasant !

But Abe's love was a queer complaint, a sort of
    tertian fever,

Each case he cured of thought the Saint a
    thorough-paced deceiver;
And soon he found, he did indeed, with all their
    whims to nourish,
That Mormonism ain't a creed where fleshly
    follies flourish.

BISHOP PETE.

Ah, right you air! A creed it is demandin' iron
    mettle!
A will that quells, as soon as riz, the biling of
    the kettle!
With wary eye, with manner deep, a spirit
    overbrimmin',
Like to a shepherd 'mong his sheep, the Saint is
    'mong his women;
And unto him they do uplift their eyes in awe
    and wonder;
His notice is a blessed gift, his anger is blue
    thunder.

No n'ises vex the holy place where dwell those
    blessed parties ;

Each missus shineth in her place, and blithe and
    meek her heart is !

They sow, they spin, they darn, they hem, their
    blessed babes they handle,

The Devil never comes to *them*, lit by that holy
    candle !

When in their midst serenely walks their
    Master and their Mentor,

They're hush'd, as when the Prophet stalks down
    holy church's centre !

They touch his robe, they do not move, those
    blessed wives and mothers,

And, when on one he shineth love, no envy fills
    the others ;

They know his perfect saintliness, and honour
    his affection—

And, if they did object, I guess he'd settle that
    objection !

BISHOP JOSS,

It ain't a passionate flat like Abe can manage
    things in *your* way!
They teased that most etarnal babe, till things
    were in a poor way.
I used to watch his thorny bed, and bust my
    sides with laughter,
Once give a female hoss her head you'll never
    stop her after.
It's one thing getting seal'd, and he was mighty
    fond of Sealing,
He'd all the human heat, d'ye see, without the
    saintly feeling.
His were the wildest set of gals that ever drove
    man silly,
Each full of freaks and fal-de-lals, as frisky as a
    filly.
One pull'd this way, and t'other that, and made
    his life a mockery,

They'd all the feelings of a cat scampaging
    'mong the crockery.
I saw Abe growing pale and thin, and well I
    knew what ail'd him—
The skunk went stealing out and in, and all his
    spirit failed him;
And tho' the tanning-yard paid well, and he
    was money-making,
His saintly home was hot as Hell, and, ah!
    how he was baking!
Why, now and then at evening-time, when his
    day's work was over,
Up this here hill he used to climb and squat
    among the clover,
And with his fishy eye he'd glare across the
    Rocky Mountains,
And wish he was away up there, among the
    heavenly fountains!
I had an aunt, Tabitha Brooks, a virgin under
    fifty,

She warn't so much for pretty looks, but she
    was wise and thrifty :

She'd seen the vanities of life, was good at
    'counts and brewin'—

Thinks I, "Here's just the sort of Wife to save
    poor Abe from ruin."

So, after fooling many a week, and showing
    him she loved him,

And seeing he was shy to *speak*, whatever
    feelings moved him,

At last I took her by the hand, and led her to
    him straightway,

One day when we could see him stand jest close
    unto the gateway.

My words were to the p'int and brief: says I,
    " My brother Clewson,

There'll be an end to all your grief, if you've got
    resolution.

Where shall you find a house that thrives with-
    out a head that's ruling ?

Here is the paragon of wives to teach those
    otners schooling !

She'll be to you not only wife, but careful as a
    mother—

A little property for life is hers; you'll share it,
    brother.

I've seen the question morn and eve within your
    eyes unspoken,

You're slow and nervous I perceive, but now—the
    ice is broken.

Here is a guardian and a guide to bless a man
    and grace him ; "

And then I to Tabitha cried, " Go in, old gal—
    embrace him ! "

STRANGER.

Why, that was acting fresh and fair ;—but Abe,
    was he as hearty ?

BISHOP JOSS.

We...ll! Abe was never anywhere against a
    female party !

At first he seemed about to run, and then we
    might have missed hiin ;
But Tabby was a tender one, she collar'd him
    and kissed him.
And round his neck she blushing hung, part
    holding, part caressing,
And murmur'd, with a faltering tongue, "O, Abe,
    I'll be a blessing."
And home they walk'd one morning, he just
    reaching to her shoulders,
And sneaking at her skirt, while she stared
    straight at all beholders.
Swinging her bonnet by the strings, and setting
    her lips tighter,
In at his door the old gal springs, her grim eyes
    growing brighter ;
And, Lord ! there was the devil to pay, and
    lightning and blue thunder,
For she was going to have her way, and hold
    the vixens under ;

They would have torn old Abe to bits, they
  were so anger-bitten,
But Tabby saved him from their fits, as a cat
  saves her kitten.

STRANGER.

It seems your patriarchal life has got its
  botherations,
And leads to much domestic strife and infinite
  vexations!
But when the ladies couldn't lodge in peace one
  house-roof under,
I thought that 'twas the saintly dodge to give
  them homes asunder?

BISHOP JOSS.

And you thought right; it is a plan by many
  here affected—
Never by *me*—I ain't the man—I'll have my will
  respected.

If all the women of *my* house can't fondly pull
    together,
And each as meek as any mouse, look out for
    stormy weather!—
No, no, I don't approve at all of humouring my
    women,
And building lots of boxes small for each one
    to grow grim in.
I teach them jealousy's a *sin*, and solitude's just
    bearish,
They nuss each other lying-in, each other's babes
    they cherish ;
It is a family jubilee, and not a selfish plea-
    sure,
Whenever one presents to me another infant
    treasure !
All ekal, all respected, each with tokens of
    affection,
They dwell together, soft of speech, beneath their
    lord's protection ;

And if by any chance I mark a spark of shindy
    raising,
I set my heel upon that spark,—before the house
    gets blazing!
Now that's what Clewson should have done, but
    couldn't, thro' his folly,
For even when Tabby's help was won, he wasn't
    much more jolly.
Altho' she stopt the household fuss, and husht
    the awful riot,
The old contrairy stupid Cuss could not enj'y
    the quiet.
His house was peaceful as a church, all solemn,
    still, and saintly;
And yet he'd tremble at the porch, and look
    about him faintly;
And tho' the place was all his own, with hat in
    hand he'd enter,
Like one thro' public buildings shown, soft
    treading down the centre.

Still, things were better than before, though
    somewhat trouble-laden,   · -

When one fine day unto his door there came a
    Yankee maiden.

"Is Brother Clewson in ?" she says; and when
    she saw and knew him,

The stranger gal to his amaze scream'd out and
    clung unto him.

Then in a voice all thick and wild, exclaim'd that
    gal unlucky,

"O Sir, I'm Jason Jones's child—he's *dead*—
    stabb'd in Kentucky!

And father's gone, and O I've come to *you*
    across the mountains."

And then the little one was dumb, and Abe's
    eyes gushed like fountains. . . .

He took that gal into his place, and kept her as
    his daughter—

Ah, mischief to her wheedling face and the bad
    wind that brought her!

BISHOP PETE.

I knew that Jones:—used to faloot about Emanci-
    pation—

It made your very toe-nails shoot to hear his
    declamation.

And when he'd made all bosoms swell with
    wonder at his vigour,

He'd get so drunk he couldn't tell a white man
    from a nigger!

Was six foot high, thin, grim, and pale,—his
    troubles can't be spoken—

Tarred, feathered, ridden on a rail, left beaten,
    bruised, and broken;

But nothing made his tongue keep still, or stopt
    his games improper,

Till, after many an awkward spill, he came the
    final cropper.

BISHOP JOSS.

. . . That gal was fourteen years of age, and sly
    with all her meekness;

It put the fam'ly in a rage, for well they knew
    Abe's weakness.
But Abe (a cuss, as I have said, that any fool
    might sit on)
Was stubborn as an ass's head, when once he
    took the fit on !
And, once he fixed the gal to take, in spite of
    their vexation,
Not all the rows on earth would break his firm
    determination.
He took the naggings as they came, he bowed
    his head quite quiet,
Still mild he was and sad and tame, and ate the
    peppery diet ;
But tho' he seemed so crush'd to be, when this
    or that one blew up,
He stuck to Jones's Legacy and school'd her till
    she grew up.
Well ! there ! the thing was said and done, and
    so far who could blame him ?

But O he was a crafty one, and sorrow couldn't
    shame him !

That gal grew up, and at eighteen was prettier
    far and neater—

There were not many to be seen about these
    parts to beat her :

Peart, brisk, bright-eyed, all trim and tight, like
    kittens fond of playing,

A most uncommon pleasant sight at pic-nic or
    at praying.

Then it became, as you'll infer, a simple public
    duty,

To cherish and look after her, considering her
    beauty;

And several Saints most great and blest now
    offer'd their protection,

And I myself among the rest felt something of
    affection.

But O the selfishness of Abe, all things it beats
    and passes !

As greedy as a two-year babe a-grasping at
    molasses!

When once those Shepherds of the flock began
    to smile and beckon,

He screamed like any fighting cock, and raised
    his comb, I reckon!

First one was floor'd, then number two, she
    wouldn't look at any;

Then *my* turn came, although I knew the
    maiden's faults were many.

" My brother Abe," says I, " I come untoe your
    house at present

To offer sister Anne a home which she will find
    most pleasant.

You know I am a saintly man, and all my ways
    are lawful "—

And in a minute he began abusing me most
    awful.

" Begone," he said, " you're like the rest,—
    wolves, wolves with greedy clutches!

Poor little lamb; but in my breast I'll shield her
  from your touches ! "

" Come, come," says I, " a gal can't stay a child
  like that for ever,

You'll *hev* to seal the gal some day ; " but Abe
  cried fiercely, " Never ! "

Says I, " Perhaps it's in your view *yourself* this
  lamb to gather ? "

And " If it is, what's that to *you?* " he cried ;
  " but I'm her father !

You get along, I know your line, it's crushing,
  bullying, wearing,

You'll never seal a child of mine, so go, and
  don't stand staring ! "

This was the man once mild in phiz as any
  farthing candle—

A hedgehog now, his quills all riz, whom no
  one dared to handle !

But O I little guessed his deal, nor tried to
  circumvent it,

I never thought he'd dare to *seal* another ; but
 he meant it !

Yes, managed Brigham on the sly, for fear his
 plans miscarried,

And long before we'd time to cry, the two were
 sealed and married.

BISHOP PETE.

Well, you've your consolation now—he's pun-
 ished clean, I'm thinking,

He's ten times deeper in the slough, up to his
 neck and sinking.

There's vinegar in Abe's pale face enough to
 sour a barrel,

Goes crawling up and down the place, neglect-
 ing his apparel,

Seems to have lost all heart and soul, has fits of
 absence shocking—

His home is like a rabbit's hole when weasels
 come a-knocking.

F

And now and then, to put it plain, while falling
    daily sicker,
I think he tries to float his pain by copious goes
    of liquor.

Bishop Joss.

Yes, that's the end of selfishness, it leads to
    long vexation—
No man can pity Abe, I guess, who knows his
    situation ;
And, Stranger, if this man you meet, don't take
    him for a sample,
Although he speaks you fair and sweet, he's set
    a vile example.
Because you see him ill at ease, at home, and
    never hearty,
Don't think these air the tokens, please, of a
    real saintly party !
No, he's a failure, he's a sham, a scandal to our
    nation,

Not fit to lead a single lamb, unworthy of his
    station ;

No ! if you want a Saint to see, who rules lambs
    when he's got 'em,

Just cock your weather-eye at *me,* or Brother
    Shufflebotham.

We don't go croaking east and west, afraid of
    women's faces,

We bless and we air truly blest in our domestic .
    places ;

We air religious, holy men, happy our folds to
    gather,

Each is a loyal citizen, also a husband—rather.

But now with talk you're dry and hot, and
    weary with your ride here,

Jest come and see *my* fam'ly lot,—they're waiting
    tea inside here.

WITHIN THE CITY.—SAINT ABE AND THE SEVEN.

Sister Tabitha, thirty odd,
Rising up with a stare and a nod;
Sister Amelia, sleepy and mild,
Freckled, Dudu-ish, suckling a child;
Sister Fanny, pert and keen,
Sister Emily, solemn and lean,
Sister Mary, given to tears,
Sister Sarah, with wool in her ears;--
All appearing like tapers wan
In the mellow sunlight of Sister Anne.

With a tremulous wave of his hand, the Saint
Introduces the household quaint,

And sinks on a chair and looks around,
As the dresses rustle with snakish sound,
As curtsies are bobb'd, and eyes cast down
Some with a simper, some with a frown,
And Sister Anne, with a fluttering breast,
Stands trembling and peeping behind the rest.

Every face but one has been
Pretty, perchance, at the age of eighteen,
Pert and pretty, and plump and bright ;
But now their fairness is faded quite,
And every feature is fashion'd here
To a flabby smile, or a snappish sneer.
Before the stranger they each assume
A false fine flutter and feeble bloom,
And a little colour comes into the cheek
When the eyes meet mine, as I sit and speak :
But there they sit and look at me,
Almost withering visibly,

And languidly tremble and try to blow—
Six pale roses all in a row!

Six ? ah, yes ; but at hand sits one,
The seventh, still full of the light of the sun.
Though her colour terribly comes and goes,
Now white as a lily, now red as a rose,
So sweet she is, and so full of light,
That the rose seems soft, and the lily bright.
Her large blue eyes, with a tender care,
Steal to her husband unaware,
And whenever he feels them he flushes red,
And the trembling hand goes up to his head !
Around those dove-like eyes appears
A redness as of recent tears.
Alone she sits in her youth's fresh bloom
In a dark corner of the room,
And folds her hands, and does not stir,
And the others scarcely look at her,

But crowding together, as if by plan,
Draw further and further from Sister Anne.

I try to rattle along in chat,
Talking freely of this and that—
The crops, the weather, the mother-land,
Talk a baby could understand;
And the faded roses, faint and meek,
Open their languid lips to speak,
But in various sharps and flats, all low,
Give a lazy " yes " or a sleepy " no."
Yet now and then Tabitha speaks,
Snapping her answer with yellow cheeks,
And fixing the Saint who is sitting by
With the fish-like glare of her glittering eye,
Whenever the looks of the weary man
Stray to the corner of Sister Anne.

Like a fountain in a shady place
Is the gleam of the sadly shining face—

A fresh spring whither the soul might turn,

When the road is rough, and the hot sands
    burn ;

Like a fount, or a bird, or a blooming tree,

To a weary spirit is such as she !

And Brother Abe, from his easy chair,

Looks thither by stealth with an aching care,

And in spite of the dragons that guard the
    brink

Would stoop to the edge of the fount, I think,

And drink ! and drink !

"Drink? Stuff and fiddlesticks," you cry,

Matron reader with flashing eye :

" Isn't the thing completely *his*,

His wife, his mistress, whatever you please ?

Look at her! Dragons and fountains! Absurd !"

Madam, I bow to every word ;

But truth is truth, and cannot fail,

And this is quite a veracious tale.

More like a couple of lovers shy,
Who flush and flutter when folk arc by,
Were man and wife, or (in another
And holier parlance) sister and brother.
As a man of the world I noticed it,
And it made me speculate a bit,
For the situation was to my mind
A phenomenon of a curious kind—
A person in love with his *wife*, 'twas clear,
But afraid, when another soul was near,
Of showing his feelings in any way
Because—there would be the Devil to pay!

The Saint has been a handsome fellow,
Clear-eyed, fresh-skinn'd, if a trifle yellow,
And his face though somewhat soft and plain
Ends in a towering mass of brain.

His locks, though still an abundant crop,
Are thinning a little at the top,

But you only notice here and there
The straggling gleam of a silver hair.
A man by nature rolled round and short,
Meant for the Merry Andrew's sport,
But sober'd down by the wear and tear
Of business troubles and household care :
Quiet, reticent, gentle, kind,
Of amorous heart and extensive mind,
A Saint devoid of saintly sham,
Is little Brother Abraham.

Brigham's right hand he used to be—
Mild though he seems, and simple, and free ;
Sound in the ways of the world, and great
In planning potent affairs of state ;
Not bright, nor bumptious, you must know,
Too retiring for popular show,
But known to conceive on a startling scale
Gigantic plans that never fail ;

To hold with a certain secret sense
The Prophet under his influence,
To be, I am led to understand,
The Brain, while the Prophet is the Hand,
And to see his intellectual way
Thro' moral dilemmas of every day,
By which the wisest are led astray.

Here's the Philosopher !—here he sits,
Here, with his vaguely wandering wits,
Among the dragons, as I have said,
Smiling, and holding his hand to his head.
What mighty thoughts are gathering now
Behind that marble mass of brow ?
What daring schemes of polity
To set the popular conscience free,
And bless humanity, planneth he ?
His talk is idle, a surface-gleam,
The ripple on the rest of the stream,

But his thoughts—ah, his *thoughts*—where do
    they fly,
While the wretched roses under his eye
Flutter and peep ? and in what doth his plan
Turn to the counsel of Sister Anne ?
For his eyes give ever a questioning look,
And the little one in her quiet nook
Flashes an answer, and back again
The question runs to the Brother's brain,
And the lights of speculation flit
Over his face and trouble it.

Follow his eyes once more, and scan
The fair young features of Sister Anne :
Frank and innocent, and in sooth
Full of the first fair flush of youth.
Quite a child—nineteen years old ;
Not gushing, and self-possessed, and bold,
Like our Yankee women at nineteen,
But low of voice, and mild of mien—

More like the fresh young fruit you see
In the mother-land across the sea—
More like that rosiest flower on earth,
A blooming maiden of English birth.
Such as we find them yet awhile
Scatter'd about the homely Isle,
Not yet entirely eaten away
By the canker-novel of the day,
Or curling up and losing their scent
In a poisonous dew from the Continent.

There she sits, in her quiet nook,
Still bright tho' sadden'd; and while I look,
My heart is filled and my eyes are dim,
And I hate the Saint when I turn to him!
Ogre! Blue Beard! Oily and sly!
His meekness a cheat, his quiet a lie!
A roaring lion he'll walk the house
Tho' now he crouches like any mouse!
Had not he pluck'd enough and to spare
Of roses like these set fading there,

But he must seek to cajole and kiss .
Another yet, and a child like this ?
A maid on the stalk, just panting to prove
The honest joy of a virgin love ;
A girl, a baby, an innocent child,
To be caught by the first man's face that smiled !
Scarce able the difference to fix
Of polygamy and politics !
Led to the altar like a lamb,
And sacrificed to the great god *Sham !*
Deluded, martyr'd, given to woe,
Last of seven who have perish'd so ;
For who can say but the flowers I see
Were once as rosy and ripe as she ?

Already the household worm has begun
To feed on the cheeks of the little one ;
Already her spirit, fever-fraught,
Droops to the weight of its own thought ;

Already she saddens and sinks and sighs,
Watched by the jealous dragonish eyes.
Even Amelia, sleepy and wan,
Sharpens her orbs as she looks at Anne ;
While Sister Tabby, when she can spare.
Her gaze from the Saint in his easy-chair,
Fixes her with a gorgon glare.

All is still and calm and polite,
The Sisters bolster themselves upright,
And try to smile, but the atmosphere
Is charged with thunder and lightning here.
Heavy it seems, and close and warm,
Like the air before a summer storm ;
And at times,—as in that drowsy dream
Preluding thunder, all sounds will seem.
Distinct and ominously clear,
And the far-off cocks seem crowing near ; —
Ev'n so in the pauses of talk, each breast
Is strangely conscious of the rest,

And the tick of the watch of Abe the Saint
Breaks on the air, distinct though faint,
Like the ticking of his heart!

                      I rise
To depart, still glancing with piteous eyes
On Sister Anne; and I find her face
Turn'd questioning still to the same old place—
The face of the Saint. I stand and bow,
Curtsies again are bobbing now,
Dresses rustling. . . I know no more
Till the Saint has led me to the door,
And I find myself in a day-dream dim,
Just after shaking hands with him,
Standing and watching him sad and slow
Into the dainty dwelling go,
With a heavy sigh, and his hand to his head.

. . . Hark, *distant thunder!*—'tis as I said :
The air was far too close ;—at length
The Storm is breaking in all its strength.

III

PROMENADE—MAIN STREET, UTAH.

THE STRANGER.

Along the streets they're throinging, walking,
Clad gaily in their best and talking,
　　Women and children quite a crowd;
The bright sun overhead is blazing,
The people sweat, the dust they're raising
　　Arises like a golden cloud.
Still out of every door they scatter,
Laughing and light.   Pray what's the matter,
　　That such a flock of folks I see?

G

A LOUNGER.

They're off to hear the Prophet patter,
   This yer's a day of jubilee.

VOICES.

Come along, we're late I reckon. . .
There's our Matt, I see him beckon. . .
How d'ye do, marm? glad to meet you. . .
Silence, Hiram, or I'll beat you. . .
Emm, there's brother Jones a-looking. . .
Here's warm weather, how I'm cooking!

STRANGER.

Afar the hills arise with cone and column
Into a sky of brass serene and solemn;
And underneath their shadow in one haze
Of limpid heat the great salt waters blaze,
While faint and filmy through the sultry veil
The purple islands on their bosom sail

Like floating clouds of dark fantastic air.
How strangely sounds (while 'mid the Indian
    glare
Moves the gay crowd of people old and young)
The bird-like chirp of the old Saxon tongue!
The women seem half weary and half gay,
Their eyes droop in a melancholy way,—
I have not seen a merry face to-day.

A Bishop.

Thet's a smart hoss you're riding, brother!
    How are things looking, down with you?

Second Bishop.

Not over bright with one nor 'tother,
    Taters are bad, tomatoes blue.
You've heer'd of Brother Simpson's losses?—
    Buried his wife and spiled his hay.
And the three best of Hornby's hosses
    Some Injin cuss has stol'n away.

VOICES.

Zoë, jest fix up my gown. . .
There's my hair a-coming down. . .
Drat the babby, he's so crusty—
It's the heat as makes him thusty. . .
Come along, I'm almost sinking. . .
There's a stranger, and he's winking.

STRANGER.

That was a fine girl with the grey-hair'd lady,
How shining were her eyes, how true and
    steady,
Not drooping down in guilty Mormon fashion,
But shooting at the soul their power and passion.
That's a big fellow, six foot two, not under,
But how he struts, and looks as black as thunder,
Half glancing round at his poor sheep to scare
    'em—
Six, seven, eight, nine,—O Abraham, what a
    harem!

All berry brown, but looking scared as may be,
And each one but the oldest with a baby.

A GIRL.

Phœbe!

ANOTHER.

Yes, Grace!

FIRST GIRL.

      Don't seem to notice, dear,
That Yankee from the camp again is here,
Making such eyes, and following on the sly,
And coughing now and then to show he's nigh.

SECOND GIRL.

Who's that along with him—the little scamp
    Shaking his hair and nodding with a smile?

FIRST GIRL.

Guess he's some new one just come down to
camp.

SECOND GIRL.

Isn't he handsome?

FIRST GIRL.

No; the first's my style!

STRANGER.

If my good friends, the Saints, could get their
    will,
These Yankee officers would fare but ill;
Wherever they approach the folk retire,
As if from veritable coals of fire;
With distant bow, set lips, and half-hid frown,
The Bishops pass them in the blessed town;
The women come behind like trembling sheep,
Some freeze to ice, some blush and steal a peep.
And often, as a band of maidens gay
Comes up, each maid ceases to talk and play,
Droops down her eyes, and does not look their
    way;

But after passing where the youngsters pine,
All giggle as at one concerted sign,
And tripping on with half-hush'd merry cries,
Look boldly back with laughter in their eyes!

VOICES.

Here we are, . . how folk are pushing . . .
Mind the babby in the crushing. . .
Pheemy! . . Yes, John! . . Don't go staring
At that Yankee—it's past bearing.
Draw your veil down while he passes,
Reckon you're as bold as brass is.

ABE CLEWSON.

[*Passing with his hand to his head, attended by his
Wives.*]

Head in a whirl, and heart in a flutter,
Guess I don't know the half that I utter.

Too much of this life is beginning to try me,

I'm like a dern'd miller the grind always nigh
    me;

Praying don't sooth me nor comfort me any,

My house is too full and my blessings too
    many—

The ways o' the wilderness puzzle me greatly.

SISTER TABITHA.

Do walk like a Christian, and keep kind o'
    stately!

And jest keep an eye on those persons behind
    you,

You call 'em your Wives, but they tease you and
    blind you;

Sister Anne's a disgrace, tho' you think her a
    martyr,

And she's tuck'd up her petticoat nigh to her
    garter.

STRANGER.

What group is this, begrim'd with dust and
    heat,
Staring like strangers in the open street ?
The women, ragged, wretched, and half dead,
Sit on the kerbstone hot and hang the head,
And clustering at their side stand children
    brown,
Weary, with wondering eyes on the fair town.
Close by in knots beside the unhorsed team
The sunburn'd men stand talking in a dream,
For the vast tracts of country left behind
Seem now a haunting mirage in the mind.
Gaunt miners folding hands upon their breasts,
    Big-jointed labourers looking ox-like down,
And sickly artizans with narrow chests
    Still pallid from the smoke of English town.
Hard by to these a group of Teutons stand,
Light-hair'd, blue-eyed, still full of Fatherland,

With water-loving Northmen, who grow gay

To see the mimic sea gleam far away.

Now to this group, with a sharp questioning
　face,

Cometh a holy magnate of the place

In decent black; shakes hands with some;
　and then

Begins an eager converse with the men:

All brighten; even the children hush their cries,

And the pale women smile with sparkling eyes.

BISHOP.

The Prophet welcomes you, and sends

His message by my mouth, my friends;

He'll see you snug, for on this shore

There's heaps of room for millions more! ..

Scotchman, I take it? .. Ah, I know

Glasgow—was there a year or so. . .

And if *you* don't from Yorkshire hail,

I'll—ah, I thought so; seldom fail.

Make yourselves snug and rest a spell,
There's liquor coming—meat as well.
All welcome!   We keep open door—
Ah, *we* don't push away the poor;
Tho' he's a fool, you understand,
Who keeps poor long in this here land.
The land of honey you behold—
Honey and milk—silver and gold!

AN ARTIZAN.

Ah, that's the style—Bess, just you hear it;
Come, come, old gal, keep up your spirit:
Silver and gold, and milk and honey,
This is the country for our money!

A GERMAN.

Es lebe die Stadt! es lebe dran!
Das heilige Leben steht mir an!

A NORTHMAN.

Taler du norske?

BISHOP.

[Shaking his head, and turning with a wink to the English.]

No, not me !

Saxon's the language of the free :
The language of the great Evangels !
The language of the Saints and Angels !
The only speech that Joseph knew !
The speech of him and Brigham too !
Only the speech by which we've thriven
Is comprehended up in Heaven ! . .
Poor heathens ! but we'll make 'em spry,
They'll talk like Christians by and by.

STRANGER.

[Strolling out of the streets.]

From east, from west, from every worn-out land,
Yearly they stream to swell this busy band.

Out of the fever'd famine of the slums,
From sickness, shame, and sorrow, Lazarus comes,
Drags his sore limbs o'er half the world and sea,
Seeking for freedom and felicity.
The sewer of ignorance and shame and loss,
Draining old Europe of its dirt and dross,
Grows the great City by the will of God;
While wondrously out of the desert sod,
Nourished with lives unclean and weary hearts
The new faith like a splendid weed upstarts.
A splendid weed! rather a fair wild-flower,
Strange to the eye in its first birth of power,
But bearing surely in its breast the seeds
Of higher issues and diviner deeds.
Changed from Sahara to a fruitful vale
Fairer than ever grew in fairy tale,
Transmuted into plenteous field and glade
By the slow magic of the white man's spade,
Grows Deseret, filling its mighty nest
Between the eastern mountains and the west, .

While—who goes there? What shape antique
　　looks down
From this green mound upon the festive town,
With tall majestic figure darkly set
Against the sky in dusky silhouette?
Strange his attire : a blanket edged with red
Wrapt royally around him ; on his head
A battered hat of the strange modern sort
Which men have christened "chimney pots" in
　　sport ;
Mocassins on his feet, fur-fringed and grand,
And a large green umbrella in his hand.
Pensive he stands with deep-lined dreamy face,
Last living remnant of the mighty race
Who on these hunting-fields for many a year
Chased the wild buffalo, and elk, and deer.
Heaven help him ! In his mien grief and despair
Seem to contend, as he stands musing there ;
Until he notices that I am nigh,
And lo ! with outstretched hands and glistening
　　eye

Swift he descends—Does he mean mischief?
  No;
He smiles and beckons as I turn to go.

INDIAN.

Me Medicine Crow. White man gib drink to
  me.
Great chief; much squaw; papoose, sah, one,
  two, three !

STRANGER.

With what a leer, half wheedling and half wink-
  ing,
The lost one imitates the act of drinking;
His nose already, to his woe and shame,
Carbuncled with the white man's liquid flame !
Well, I pull out my flask, and fill a cup
Of burning rum—how quick he gulps it up;
And in a moment in his trembling grip
Thrusts out the cup for more with thirsty lip.

But no !—already drunken past a doubt,
Degenerate nomad of the plains, get out !

[*A railway whistle sounds in the far distance.*]

Fire-hearted Demon tamed to human hand,
Rushing with smoky breath from land to land,
Screaming aloud to scare with rage and wrath
Primæval ignorance before his path,
Dragging behind him as he runs along
His lilliputian masters, pale and strong,
With melancholy sound for plain and hill
Man's last Familiar Spirit whistles shrill.

Poor devil of the plains, now spent and frail,
Hovering wildly on the fatal trail,
Pass on !—there lies thy way and thine abode,
Get out of Jonathan thy master's road.
Where ? anywhere !—he's not particular where,
So that you clear the road, he does not care;

Off, quick! clear out! ay, drink your fill and die;
And, since the Earth rejects you, try the Sky!
And see if He, who sent your white-faced
    brother
To hound and drive you from this world you
    bother,
Can find a corner for you in another!

IV.

WITHIN THE SYNAGOGUE.—SERMCNIZETII THE PROPHET.

Sisters and brothers who love the right,
    Saints whose hearts are divinely beating,
Children rejoicing in the light,
    I reckon this is a pleasant meeting.
Where's the face with a look of grief?—
    Jehovah's with us and leads the battle ;
We've had a harvest beyond belief,
    And the signs of fever have left the cattle ;
All still blesses the holy life
    Here in the land of milk and honey.

FEMININE WHISPERS.

Brother Shuttleworth's seventeenth wife, . .
  Her with the heer brushed up so funny !

THE PROPHET.

Out of Egypt hither we flew,
  Through the desert and rocky places ;
The people murmur'd, and all look'd blue,
  The bones of the martyr'd filled our traces.
Mountain and valley we crawl'd along,
  And every morning our hearts beat quicker.
Our flesh was weak, but our souls were strong,
  And we'd managed to carry some kegs of
    liquor.
At last we halted on yonder height,
  Just as the sun in the west was blinking.

FEMININE WHISPERS.

Isn't Jedge Hawkins's last a fright ? . . .
  I'm suttin that Brother Abe's been drinking!

The Prophet.

That night, my lambs, in a wondrous dream,
 I saw the gushing of many fountains;
Soon as the morning began to beam,
 Down we went from yonder mountains,
Found the water just where I thought,
 Fresh and good, though a trifle gritty,
Pitch'd our tents in the plain, and wrought
 The site and plan of the Holy City.
" Pioneers of the blest," I cried,
  "Dig, and the Lord will bless each spade-
   ful."

Feminine Whispers.

Brigham's sealed to another Bride. . .
  How worn he's gittin'! he's aging dreadful.

THE PROPHET.

This is a tale so often told,
 The theme of every eventful meeting;
Yes! you may smile and think it old;
 But yet it's a tale that will bear repeating.
That's how the City of Light began,
 That's how we founded the saintly nation,
All by the spade and the arm of man,
 And the aid of a special dispensation.
"Work" was the word when we begun,
 "Work" is the word now we have plenty.

FEMININE WHISPERS.

Heard about Sister Euphemia's son ? . .
 Sealing already, though only twenty!

THE PROPHET.

I say just now what I used to say,
 Though it moves the heathens to mock and
  laughter,

From work to prayer is the proper way—
    Labour first, and Religion after.
Let a big man, strong in body and limb,
    Come here inquiring about his Maker,
This is the question I put to him,
      " Can you grow a cabbage, or reap an
         acre ? "
What's the soul but a flower sublime,
    Grown in the earth and upspringing surely ?

FEMININE WHISPERS.

O yes ! she's hed a most dreadful time !
    Twins, both thriving, though she's so
      poorly.

THE PROPHET.

Beauty, my friends, is the crown of life,
    To the young and foolish seldom granted ;
After a youth of honest strife
    Comes the reward for which you've panted.

O blessed sight beyond compare,
    When life with its halo of light is rounded,
To see a Saint with reverend hair
    Sitting like Solomon love-surrounded !
One at his feet and one on his knee,
    Others around him, blue-eyed and dreamy !

FEMININE WHISPERS.

All very well, but as for *me*,
    My man had better !—I'd *pison* him,
      Pheemy !

THE PROPHET.

There in the gate of Paradise
    The Saint is sitting serene and hoary,
Tendrils of arms, and blossoms of eyes,
    Festoon him round in his place of glory ;
Little cherubs float thick as bees
    Round about him, and murmur " father ! "

The sun shines bright and he sits at ease,
Fruit all round for his hand to gather.
Blessed is he and for ever gay,
Floating to Heaven and adding to it!

FEMININE WHISPERS.

Thought I should have gone mad that day
He brought a second; I made him rue it!

THE PROPHET.

Sisters and Brothers by love made wise,
Remember, when Satan attempts to quell
you,
If this here Earth isn't Paradise
You'll never see it, and so I tell you.
Dig and drain, and harrow and sow,
God will bless you beyond all measure;
Labour, and meet with reward below,
For what is the end of all labour? Plea-
sure!

Labour's the vine, and pleasure's the grape,
    The one delighting, the other bearing.

FEMININE WHISPERS.

Higginson's third is losing her shape.
    She hes too many—it's dreadful wearing.

THE PROPHET.

But I hear some awakening spirit cry,
    " Labour is labour, and all men know it ;
But what is pleasure ?" and I reply,
    Grace abounding and Wives to show it !
Holy is he beyond compare
    Who tills his acres and takes his blessing,
Who sees around him everywhere
    Sisters soothing and babes caressing.
And *his* delight is Heaven's as well,
    For swells he not the ranks of the chosen ?

FEMININE WHISPERS.

Martha is growing a handsome gel. . .
    Three at a birth ?—that makes the dozen.

THE PROPHET.

Learning's a shadow, and books a jest,
    One Book's a Light, but the rest are human.
The kind of study that I think best
    Is the use of a spade and the love of a
    woman.
Here and yonder, in heaven and earth,
    By big Salt Lake and by Eden river,
The finest sight is a man of worth,
    Never tired of increasing his quiver.
He sits in the light of perfect grace
    With a dozen cradles going together !

FEMININE WHISPERS.

The babby's growing black in the face !
    Carry him out—it's the heat of the weather !

THE PROPHET.

A faithful vine at the door of the Lord,
    A shining flower in the garden of spirits,
A lute whose strings are of sweet accord,
    Such is the person of saintly merits.
Sisters and brothers, behold and strive
    Up to the level of his perfection;
Sow, and harrow, and dig, and thrive,
    Increase according to God's direction.
This is the Happy Land, no doubt,
    Where each may flourish in his vocation. . .
Brother Bantam will now give out
    The hymn of love and of jubilation.

V.

THE FALLING OF THE THUNDERBOLT.

Deep and wise beyond expression
Sat the Prophet holding session,
And his Elders, round him sitting
With a gravity befitting,
Never rash and never fiery,
Chew'd the cud of each inquiry,
Weigh'd each question and discussed it,
Sought to settle and adjust it,
Till, with sudden indication
Of a gush of inspiration,
The grave Prophet from their middle
Gave the answer to their riddle,

And the lesser lights all holy,
Round the Lamp revolving slowly,
Thought, with eyes and lips asunder,
" *Right,* we reckon, he's a wonder!"

Whether Boyes, that blessed brother,
Should be sealed unto another,
Having, tho' a Saint most steady,
Very many wives already?
Whether it was held improper,
If a woman drank, to drop her?
Whether unto Brother Fleming
Formal praise would be beseeming,
Since from three or four potatoes
(Not much bigger than his great toes)
He'd extracted, to their wonder,
Four stone six and nothing under?
Whether Bigg be reprimanded
For his conduct underhanded.

Since he'd packed his prettiest daughter
To a heathen o'er the water?
How, now Thompson had departed,
His poor widows, broken-hearted,
Should be settled? They were seven,
Sweet as cherubs up in heaven;
Three were handsome, young, and pleasant,
And had offers on at present—
Must they take them?.. These and other
Questions proffer'd by each brother,
The great Prophet ever gracious,
Free and easy, and sagacious,
Answer'd after meditation
With sublime deliberation;
And his answers were so clever
Each one whisper'd, "Well I never!"
And the lesser lights all holy,
Round the Prophet turning slowly,
Raised their reverend heads and hoary,
Thinking, "To the Prophet, glory!

Hallelujah, veneration,
Reckon that he licks creation !"

Suddenly as they sat gleaming,
On them came an unbeseeming
Murmur, tumult, and commotion,
Like the breaking of the ocean ;
And before a word was utter'd,
In rush'd one with voice that fluttered
Arms uplifted, face the colour
Of a bran-new Yankee dollar,
Like a man whose wits are addled,
Crying—"*Brother Abe's skedaddled!* "

Then those Elders fearful-hearted
Raised a loud cry and upstarted,
But the Prophet, never rising,
Said, "Be calm ! this row's surprising !"
And as each Saint sank unsinew'd
In his arm-chair he continued :

" Goodman Jones, your cheeks are yellow,
Tell thy tale, and do not bellow!
What's the reason of your crying—
Is our brother *dead ?*—or *dying ?*"

As the Prophet spake, supremely
Hushing all the strife unseemly,
Sudden in the room there entered
Shapes on whom all eyes were centred—
Six sad female figures moaning,
Trembling, weeping, and intoning,
" We are widows broken-hearted—
Abraham Clewson has departed !"

While the Saints again upleaping
Joined their voices to the weeping,
For a moment the great Prophet
Trembled, and look'd dark as Tophet.
But the cloud pass'd over lightly.
" Cease !" he cried, but sniffled slightly,

"Cease this murmur and be quiet—
Dead men won't awake with riot.
'Tis indeed a loss stupendous—
When will Heaven his equal send us?
Speak, then, of our brother cherish'd,
Was it *fits* by which he perish'd?
Or did Death come even quicker,
'Thro' a bolting horse or kicker?"

At the Prophet's question scowling,
All the Wives stood moaning, howling,
Crying wildly in a fever,
"O the villain! the deceiver!"
But the oldest stepping boldly,
Curtseying to the Session coldly,
Cried in voice like cracking thunder,
"Prophet, don't you make a blunder!
Abraham Clewson isn't dying—
Hasn't died, as you're implying

I

No! he's not the man, my brothers,
To die decently like others!
Worse! he's from your cause revolted—
Run away! ske-daddled! bolted!"

Bolted! run away! skedaddled!
Like to men whose wits are addled,
Echoed all those Lights so holy,
Round the Prophet shining slowly
And the Prophet, undissembling,
Underneath the blow sat trembling,
While the perspiration hovered
On his forehead, and he covered
With one trembling hand his features
From the gaze of smaller creatures.
Then at last the high and gifted
Cough'd and craved, with hands uplifted,
Silence. When 'twas given duly,
" This," said he, " 's a crusher truly!

Brother Clewson fall'n from glory!
I can scarce believe your story.
O my Saints, each in his station,
Join in prayer and meditation!"

Covering up each eyelid saintly
With a finger tip, prayed faintly,
Shining in the church's centre,
Their great Prophet, Lamp, and Mentor;
And the lesser Lights all holy,
Round the Lamp revolving slowly,
Each upon his seat there sitting,
With a gravity befitting,
Bowed their reverend heads and hoary,
Saying, "To the Prophet glory!
Hallelujah, veneration!
Reckon that he licks creation!"

Lastly, when the trance was ended,
And, with face where sorrow blended

Into pity and compassion,
Shone the Light in common fashion;
Forth the Brother stept who brought them
First the news which had distraught them,
And, while stood the Widows weeping,
Gave into the Prophet's keeping
A seal'd paper, which the latter
Read, as if 'twere solemn matter—
Gravely pursing lips and nodding,
While they watch'd in dark foreboding,
Till at last, with voice that quivered,
He these woeful words delivered :—

" Sisters, calm your hearts unruly,
'Tis an awful business truly;
Weeping now will save him never,
He's as good as lost for ever;
Yes, I say with grief unspoken,
Jest a pane crack'd, smash'd, and broken

In the windows of the Temple—
Crack'd 's the word—so take example !
Had he left ye one and all here
On our holy help to call here,
Fled alone from *every* fetter,
I could comprehend it better !
Flying, not with some strange lady,
But with her he had already,
With his own seal'd Wife eloping—
It's a case of craze past hoping !
List, O Saints, each in his station,
To the idiot's explanation ! "

Then, while now and then the holy
Broke the tale of melancholy
With a grunt contempt expressing,
And the widows made distressing
Murmurs of recrimination
Here and there in the narration,
The great Prophet in affliction
Read this awful Valediction !

VI

LAST EPISTLE OF ST. ABE TO THE
POLYGAMISTS.

O Brother, Prophet of the Light!—don't let my
    state distress you,
While from the depths of darkest night I cry,
    "Farewell! God bless you!"
I don't deserve a parting tear, nor even a male-
    diction,
Too weak to fill a saintly sphere, I yield to my
    affliction;
Down like a cataract I shoot into the depths
    below you,
While you stand wondering and mute, my last
    adieu I throw you;

Commending to your blessed care my well-be-
loved spouses,

My debts (there's plenty and to spare to pay
them), lands, and houses,

My sheep, my cattle, farm and fold, yea, all by
which I've thriven :

These to be at the auction sold, and to my
widows given.

Bless them ! to prize them at their worth was
far beyond my merit,

Just make them think me in the earth, a poor
departed spirit.

I couldn't bear to say good-bye, and see their
tears up-starting ;

I thought it best to pack and fly without the
pain of parting !

O tell Amelia, if she can, by careful educa-
tion,

To make her boy grow up a man of strength
and saintly station !

Tell Fanny to beware of men, and say I'm still
    her debtor—

Tho' she cut sharpish now and then, I think it
    made me better!

Let Emily still her spirit fill with holy consola-
    tions—

Seraphic soul, I hear her still a-reading " Reve-
    lations ! "

Bid Mary now to dry her tears—she's free of her
    chief bother ;

And comfort Sarah—I've my fears she's going to
    be a mother ;

And to Tabitha give for me a tender kiss of
    healing—

Guilt wrings my soul—I seem to see that well-
    known face appealing !

And now,—before my figure fades for ever from
    your vision,

Before I mingle with the shades beyond your
    light Elysian,

Now, while your faces all turn pale, and you
    raise eyes and shiver,
Let me a round unvarnish'd tale (as Shakspere
    says) deliver ;
And let there be a warning text in my most
    shameful story,
When some poor sheep, perplext and vext, goes
    seeking too much glory.
O Brigham, think of my poor fate, a scandal to
    beholders,
And don't again put too much weight before
    you've tried the shoulders !

Though I'd the intellectual gift, and knew the
    rights and reasons ;
Though I could trade, and save, and shift,
    according to the seasons ;
Though I was thought a clever man, and was at
    spouting splendid,—
Just think how finely I began, and see how all
    has ended !

In *principle* unto this hour I'm still a holy
    being—

But oh, how poorly is my power proportion'd to
    my seeing!

You've all the logic on your side, you're right in
    each conclusion,

And yet how vainly have I tried, with eager
    resolution!

My will was good, I felt the call, although my
    strength was meagre,

There wasn't one among you all to serve the
    Lord more eager!

I never tired in younger days of drawing lambs
    unto me,

My lot was one to bless and praise, the fire of
    faith thrill'd through me.

And *you*, believing I was strong, smiled on me
    like a father,—

Said, " Blessëd be this man, though young, who
    the sweet lambs doth gather!"

At first it wás a time full blest, and all my
    earthy pleasure

Was gathering lambs unto my breast to cherish
    and to treasure;

Ay, one by one, for heaven's sake, my female
    flock I found me,

Until one day I did awake and heard them
    bleating round me,

And there was sorrow in their eyes, and mute
    reproach and wonder,

For they perceived to their surprise their Shep-
    herd was a blunder.

O Brigham, think of it and weep, my firm and
    saintly Master—

The Pastor trembled at his Sheep, the Sheep despised
    the Pastor!

O listen to the tale of dread, thou Light that
    shines so brightly—

Virtue's a horse that drops down dead if over-
    loaded slightly!

She s all the *will,* she wants to go, she'd carry
    every tittle;

But when you see her flag and blow, just ease
    her of a little !

One wife for me was near enough, *two* might
    have fixed me neatly,

Three made me shake, *four* made me puff, *five*
    settled me completely,—

But when the *sixth* came, though I still was
    glad and never grumbled,

I took the staggers, kick'd, went ill, and in the
    traces tumbled!

Ah, well may I compare my state unto a beast's
    position—

Unfit to bear a saintly weight, I sank and lost
    condition ;

I lack'd the moral nerve and thew, to fill so fine
    a station—

Ah, if I'd had a head like you, and your deter-
    mination !

Instead of going in and out, like a superior
party,

I was too soft of heart, no doubt, too open, and
too hearty.

When I *began* with each young sheep I was too
free and loving,

Not being strong and wise and deep, I set her
feelings moving ;

And so, instead of noticing the gentle flock in
common,

I waken'd up that mighty thing—the Spirit of a
Woman.

Each got to think me, don't you see,—so foolish
was the feeling,—

Her own especial property, which all the rest
were stealing !

And, since I could not give to each the whole of
my attention,

All came to grief, and parts of speech too delicate to mention !

Bless them! they loved me far too much, they
 erred in their devotion,
I lack'd the proper saintly touch, subduing mere
 emotion :—
The solemn air sent from the skies, so cold, so
 tranquillising,
That on the female waters lies, and keeps the
 same from rising,
But holds them down all smooth and bright,
 and, if some wild wind storms 'em,
Comes like a cold frost in the night, and into *ice*
 transforms 'em!

And there, between ourselves, I see the diffi-
 culty growing,
Since most men are as meek as me, too passionate and glowing;
They cannot in *your* royal way dwell like a
 guest from Heaven
Within this tenement of clay, which for the Soul
 is given;

They cannot like a blessed guest come calm and
    strong into it,

Eating and drinking of its best, and calmly
    gazing thro' it.

No, every mortal's not a Saint, and truly very
    few are,

So weak they are, they cannot paint what holy
    men like you are.

Instead of keeping well apart the Flesh and
    Spirit, brother,

And making one with cunning art the nigger of
    the other,

They muddle and confuse the two, they mix and
    twist and mingle,

So that it takes a cunning view to make out
    either single.

The Soul gets mingled with the Flesh beyond all
    separation,

The Body holds it in a mesh of animal sensa-
    tion ;

The poor bewilder'd Being, grown a thing in
    nature double,
Half light and soul, half flesh and bone, is given
    up to trouble.
He thinks the instinct of the clay, the glowings
    of the Spirit,
And when the Spirit has her say, inclines the
    Flesh to hear it.
The slave of every passing whim, the dupe of
    every devil,
Inspired by every female limb to love, and light,
    and revel,
Impulsive, timid, weak, or strong, as Flesh or
    Spirit makes him,
The lost one wildly moans along till mischief
    overtakes him ;
And when the Soul has fed upon the Flesh till
    life's spring passes,
Finds strength and health and comfort gone—
    the way of last year's grasses,

And the poor Soul is doom'd to bow, in deep
    humiliation,
Within a place that isn't now a decent habitation.

No! keep the Soul and Flesh apart in pious
    resolution,
Don't let weak flutterings of the heart lead you
    to *my* confusion!
But let the Flesh be as the *horse*, the Spirit as
    the *rider*,
And use the snaffle first of course, and ease her
    up and guide her;
And if she's going to resist, and won't let none
    go past her,
Just take the *curb* and give a twist, and show
    her you're the Master.
The Flesh is but a temporal thing, and Satan's
    strength is in it,
Use it, but conquer it, and bring its vice dow
    every minute!

K

Into a woman's arms don't fall, as if you meant
to *stay* there,
*Just come as if you'd made a call, and idly found
your way there;*
Don't praise her too much to her face, but keep
her calm and quiet,—
Most female illnesses take place thro' far too
warm a diet;
Unto her give your fleshly kiss, calm, kind, and
patronising,
Then—soar to your own sphere of bliss, before
her heart gets rising !
Don't fail to let her see full clear, how in your
saintly station
The Flesh is but your nigger here obeying your
dictation ;
And tho' the Flesh be e'er so warm, your Soul
the weakness smothers
Of loving any female form much better than the
others !

O Brigham, I can see you smile to hear the
    Devil preaching ;—

Well, I can praise your perfect style, tho' far
    beyond my reaching.

Forgive me, if in shame and grief I vex you with
    digression,

And let me come again in brief to my own dark
    confession.

The world of men divided is into *two portions*,
    brother,

The first are Saints, so high in bliss that they the
    Flesh can smother;

God meant them from fair flower to flower to
    flutter, smiles bestowing,

Tasting the sweet, leaving the sour, just hover-
    ing,—and going.

The second are a different set, just *halves* of
    perfect spirits,

Going about in bitter fret, of uncompleted
    merits,

Till they discover, here or there, their *other half*
    (or woman),
Then these two join, and make a Pair, and so
    increase the human.
The second Souls inferior are, a lower spirit-
    order,
Born 'neath a less auspicious star, and taken by
    soft sawder;—
And if they do not happen here to find their fair
    Affinity,
They come to grief and doubt and fear, and end
    in asininity;
And if they try the blessed game of those
    superior to them,
They're very quickly brought to shame,—their
    passions so undo them.
In some diviner sphere, perhaps, they'll look and
    grow more holy,—
Meantime they're vessels Sorrow taps and grim
    Remorse sucks slowly.

Now, Brigham, *I* was made, you see, one of
those *lower* creatures,

Polygamy was not for me, altho' I joined its
preachers.

Instead of, with a wary eye, seeking the one
who waited,

And sticking to her, wet or dry, because the
thing was fated,

I snatch'd the first whose beauty stirred my soul
with tender feeling !

And then another ! then a third ! and so continued Sealing !

And duly, after many a smart, discovered,
sighing faintly,

I *hadn't* found my missing part, and *wasn't*
strong and saintly !

O they were far too good for me, altho' their
zeal betrayed them ;—

Unfortunately, don't you see, heaven for some
other made them :

Each would a downright blessing be, and Peace
 would pitch the tent for her,
If " she " could only find the " he " originally
 meant for her !

Well, Brother, after many years of bad domestic
 diet,
One morning I woke up in tears, still weary and
 unquiet,
And (speaking figuratively) lo ! beside my bed
 stood smiling
The Woman, young and virgin snow, but beckon-
 ing and beguiling.
I started up, my wild eyes rolled, I knew her,
 and stood sighing,
My thoughts throng'd up like bees of gold out of
 the smithy flying.
And as she stood in brightness there, familiar,
 tho' a stranger,
I looked at her in dumb despair, and trembled
 at the danger.

But, Brother Brigham, don't you think the
    Devil could so undo me,

That straight I rushed the cup to drink too late
    extended to me.

No, for I hesitated long, ev'n when I found she
    loved me,

And didn't seem to think it wrong when love
    and passion moved me.

O Brigham, you're a Saint above, and know not
    the sensation

The ecstasy, the maddening love, the rapturous
    exultation,

That fills a man of lower race with wonder past
    all speaking,

When first he finds in one sweet face the Soul he
    has been seeking !

When two immortal beings glow in the first
    fond revealing,

And their inferior natures know the luxury of
    feeling !

But ah, I had already got a quiver-full of blessing,
Had blundered, tho' I knew it not, six times
 beyond redressing,
And surely it was time to stop, tho' still my lot
 was lonely :
My house was like a cobbler's shop, full, tho'
 with "misfits" only.

And so I *should* have stopt, I swear, the
 wretchedest of creatures,
Rather than put one mark of care on her
 belovéd features :
But that it happen'd Sister Anne (ah, now the
 secret's flitted !)
Was left in this great world of man unto my
 care committed.
Her father, Jason Jones, was dead, a man whose
 faults were many,
"O, be a father, Abe," he said, "to my poor
 daughter, Annie !"

And so I promised, so she came an Orphan to
    this city,

And set my foolish heart in flame with mingled
    love and pity;

And as she prettier grew each day, and throve
    'neath my protection,

I saw the Saints did cast her way some tokens of
    affection.

O, Brigham, pray forgive me now;—envy and
    love combining,

I hated every saintly brow, benignantly in-
    clining!

Sneered at their motives, mocked the cause,
    went wild and sorrow-laden,

And saw Polygamy's vast jaws a-yawning for
    the maiden.

Why *not*, you say? Ah, yes, why not, from
    your high point of vision;

But I'm of an inferior lot, beyond the light
    Elysian.

I tore my hair, whined like a whelp, I loved her
    to distraction,

I saw the danger, knew the help, yet trembled
    at the action.

At last I came to you, my friend, and told my
    tender feeling;

You said, " Your grief shall have an end—this is
    a case for Sealing ;

And since you have deserved so well, and made
    no heinous blunder,

Why, brother Abraham, *take* the gel, but mind
    you keep her under."

Well! then I went to Sister Anne, my inmost
    heart unclothing,

Told her my feelings like a man, concealing
    next to nothing,

Explain'd the various characters of those I had
    already,

The various tricks and freaks and stirs peculiar
    to each lady,

And, finally, when all was clear, and hope
    seem'd to forsake me,
" There! it's a wretched chance, my dear—you
    leave me, or you take me."
Well, Sister Annie look'd at me, *her* inmost
    heart revealing
(Women are very weak, you see, inferior, full of
    feeling),
Then, thro' her tears outshining bright, " I'll
    never never leave you!
" O Abe," she said, " my love, my light, why
    should I pain or grieve you?
I do not love the way of life you have so sadly
    chosen,
I'd rather be a single wife than one in half a
    dozen;
But now you cannot change your plan, tho'
    health and spirit perish,
And I shall never see a man but you to love and
    cherish.

Take me, I'm yours, and O, my dear, don't
    think I miss your merit,
I'll try to help a little here your true and loving
    spirit."
" Reflect, my love," I said, " once more," with
    bursting heart, half crying,
" Two of the girls cut very sore, and most of
    them are trying!"
And then that gentle-hearted maid kissed me
    and bent above me,
" O Abe," she said, " don't be afraid,—I'll try to
    make them *love* me!"

Ah well! I scarcely stopt to ask myself, till all
    was over,
How precious tough would be her task who
    made those dear souls love her!
But I was seal'd to Sister Anne, and straight-
    way to my wonder
A series of events began which show'd me all
    my blunder.

Brother, don't blame the souls who erred thro'
  their excess of feeling—
So angrily their hearts were stirred by my last
  act of sealing;
But in a moment they forgot the quarrels they'd
  been wrapt in,
And leagued together in one lot, with Tabby for
  the Captain.
Their little tiffs were laid aside, and all com-
  bined together,
Preparing for the gentle Bride the blackest sort
  of weather.
It wasn't *feeling* made them flout poor Annie in
  that fashion,
It wasn't love turn'd inside out, it wasn't jealous
  passion,
It wasn't that they cared for *me*, or any other
  party,
Their hearts and sentiments were free, their ap-
  petites were hearty.

But when the pretty smiling face came blossom-
    ing and blooming,

Like sunshine in a shady place the fam'ly Vault-
    illuming,

It naturally made them grim to see its sunny
    colour,

While like a row of tapers dim by daylight, they
    grew duller.

She tried her best to make them kind, she
    coaxed and served them dumbly,

She watch'd them with a willing mind, deferred
    to them most humbly ;

Tried hard to pick herself a friend, but found her
    arts rejected,

And fail'd entirely in her end, as one might
    have expected.

But, Brother, tho' I'm loathe to add one word to
    criminate them,

I think their conduct was too bad,—it almost
    made me hate them.

Ah me, the many nagging ways of women are
    amazing,
Their cleverness solicits. praise, their cruelty is
    crazing !
And Sister Annie hadn't been a single day their
    neighbour,
Before a baby could have seen her life would be
    a labour.
But bless her little loving heart, it kept its
    sorrow hidden,
And if the tears began to start, suppressed the
    same unbidden.
She tried to smile, and smiled her best, till I
    thought sorrow silly,
And kept in her own garden nest, and lit it like
    a lily.
O I should waste your time for days with talk
    like this at present,
If I described her thousand ways of making
    things look pleasant !

But, bless you, 'twere as well to try, when
    thunder's at its dire work,
To clear the air, and light the sky, by penny-
    worths of firework.
These gentle ways to hide her woe and make
    my life a blessing,
Just made the after darkness grow more gloomy
    and depressing.
Taunts, mocks, and jeers, coldness and sneers,
    insult and trouble daily,
A thousand stabs that brought the tears, all
    these she cover'd gaily;
But when her fond eyes fell on *me*, the light of
    love to borrow,
And Sister Anne began to see *I knew* her secret
    sorrow,
All of a sudden like a mask the loving cheat
    forsook her,
And reckon I had all my task, for *illness* over-
    took her.

She took to bed, grew sad and thin, seem'd like
    a spirit flying,
Smiled thro' her tears when I went in, but when
    I left fell crying;
And as she languish'd in her bed, as weak and
    wan as water,
I thought of what her father said, "Take care of
    my dear daughter!"
Then I look'd round with secret eye upon her
    many Sisters,
And close at hand I saw them lie, ready for use
    —like blisters;
They seemed with secret looks of glee, to keep
    their wifely station:
They set their lips and sneer'd at me, and
    watch'd the situation.
O Brother, I can scarce express the agony of
    those moments,
I fear your perfect saintliness, and dread your
    cutting comments!

I prayed, I wept, I moan'd, I cried, I anguish'd
    night and morrow,
I watch'd and waited, sleepless-eyed, beside
    that bed of sorrow.

At last I knew, in those dark days of sorrow
    and disaster,
Mine wasn't soil where you could raise a Saint
    up, or a Pastor;
In spite of careful watering, and tilling night
    and morning,
The weeds of vanity would spring without a
    word of warning.
I was and ever must subsist, labell'd on every
    feature,
A wretched poor *Monogamist*, a most inferior
    creature—
Just half a soul, and half a mind, a blunder and
    abortion,
Not finish'd half till I could find the other
    missing portion!

And gazing on that missing part which I at last
    had found out,
I murmur'd with a burning heart, scarce strong
    to get the sound out,
" If from the greedy clutch of Fate I save this
    chief of treasures,
I will no longer hesitate, but take decided mea-
    sures !
A poor monogamist like me can *not* love half a
    dozen,
Better by far, then, set them free ! and take the
    Wife I've chosen !
Their love for me, of course, is small, a very
    shadowy tittle,
They will not miss my face at all, or miss it very
    little.
I can't undo what I have done, by my forlorn
    embraces,
And call the brightness of the sun again into
    their faces ;

But I *can* save one spirit true, confiding and
    unthinking,

From slowly curdling to a shrew or into swine-
    dom sinking."

These were my bitter words of woe, my fears
    were so distressing,

Not that I would reflect—O no!—on any living
    blessing.

Thus, Brother, I resolved, and when she rose,
    still frail and sighing,

I kept my word like better men, and bolted,—
    and I'm flying.

Into oblivion I haste, and leave the world be-
    hind me,

Afar unto the starless waste, where not a soul
    shall find me.

I send my love, and Sister Anne joins cordially,
    agreeing

I never was the sort of man for your high state
    of being;

Such as I am, she takes me, though; and after
    years of trying,

From Eden hand in hand we go, like our first
    parents flying;

And like the bright sword that did chase the
    first of sires and mothers,

Shines dear Tabitha's flaming face, surrounded
    by the others:

Shining it threatens there on high, above the
    gates of heaven,

And faster at the sight we fly, in naked shame,
    forth-driven.

Nothing of all my worldly store I take, 'twould
    be improper,

I go a pilgrim, strong and poor, without a single
    copper.

Unto my Widows I outreach my property com-
    pletely.

There's modest competence for each, if it is
    managed neatly.

That, Brother, is a labour left to your sagacious
keeping;—
Comfort them, comfort the bereft! I'm good as
dead and sleeping!
A fallen star, a shooting light, a portent and an
omen,
A moment passing on the sight, thereafter seen
by no men!
I go, with backward-looking face, and spirit
rent asunder.
O may you prosper in your place, for you're a
shining wonder!
So strong, so sweet, so mild, so good!—by
Heaven's dispensation,
Made Husband to a *multitude* and Father to a
nation!
May all the saintly life ensures increase and
make you stronger!
Humbly and penitently yours,

A. CLEWSON (*Saint no longer*).

THE FARM IN THE VALLEY—SUNSET.

(1871.)

THE FARM IN THE VALLEY.

STILL the saintly City stands,
Wondrous work of busy hands:
Still the lonely City thrives,
Rich in worldly goods and wives,
And with thrust-out jaw and set
Teeth, the Yankee threatens yet—
Half admiring and half riled,
Oft by bigger schemes beguiled,
Turning off his curious stare
To communities elsewhere,
Always with unquiet eye
Watching Utah on the sly.

Long the City of the Plain
Left its image on my brain :
White kiosks and gardens bright
Rising in a golden light ;
Busy figures everywhere
Bustling bee-like in the glare ;
And from dovecots in green places,
Peep'd out weary women's faces,
Flushing faint to a thin cry
From the nursery hard by.
And the City in my thought
Slept fantastically wrought,
Till the whole began to seem
Like a curious Eastern dream,
Like the pictures strange we scan
In the tales Arabian :
Tales of magic art and sleight,
Cities rising in a night,
And of women richly clad,
Dark-eyed, melancholy, sad,

Ever with a glance uncertain,
Trembling at the purple curtain,
Lest behind the black slave stand
With the bowstring in his hand ;—
Happy tales, within whose heart
Founts of weeping eyes upstart,
Told, to save her pretty head,
By Scheherazad in bed !

All had faded and grown faint,
Save the figure of the Saint
Who that memorable night
Left the Children of the Light,
Flying o'er the lonely plain
From his lofty sphere of pain
Oft his gentle face would flit
O'er my mind and puzzle it,
Ever waking up meanwhile
Something of a merry smile,

Whose quick light illumined me
During many a reverie,
When I puffed my weed alone.

Faint and strange the face had grown,
Tho' for five long years or so
I had watched it come and go,
When, on busy thoughts intent,
I into New England went,
And one evening, riding slow
By a River that I know,
(Gentle stream! I hide thy name,
Far too modest thou for fame!)
I beheld the landscape swim
In the autumn hazes dim,
And from out the neighbouring dales
Heard the thumping of the flails.

All was hush'd; afar away
(As a novelist would say)

Sank the mighty orb of day,
Staring with a hazy glow
On the purple plain below,
Where (like burning embers shed
From the sunset's glowing bed,
Dying out or burning bright,
Every leaf a blaze of light)
Ran the maple swamps ablaze ;
Everywhere amid the haze,
Floating strangely in the air,
Farms and homesteads gather'd fair ;
And the River rippled slow
Thro' the marshes green and low,
Spreading oft as smooth as glass
As it fringed the meadow grass,
Making 'mong the misty fields
Pools like golden gleaming shields.

Thus I walked my steed along,
Humming a low scrap of song,

Watching with an idle eye
White clouds in the dreamy sky
Sailing with me in slow pomp.
In the bright flush of the swamp,
While his dogs bark'd in the wood,
Gun in hand the sportsman stood ;
And beside me, wading deep,
Stood the angler half asleep,
Figure black against the gleam
Of the bright pools of the stream ;
Now and then a wherry brown
With the current drifted down
Sunset-ward, and as it went
Made an oar-splash indolent ;
While with solitary sound,
Deepening the silence round,
In a voice of mystery
Faintly cried the chickadee.

Suddenly the River's arm
Rounded, and a lonely Farm
Stood before me blazing red
To the bright blaze overhead;
In the homesteads at its side,
Cattle lowed and voices cried,
And from out the shadows dark
Came a mastiff's measured bark.
Fair and fat stood the abode
On the path by which I rode,
And a mighty orchard, strown
Still with apple-leaves wind-blown,
Raised its branches gnarl'd and bare
Black against the sunset air,
And with greensward deep and dim,
Wander'd to the River's brim.

Close beside the orchard walk
Linger'd one in quiet talk

With a man in workman's gear.
As my horse's feet drew near,
The labourer nodded rough "good-day,"
Turned his back and loung'd away.
Then the first, a plump and fat
Yeoman in a broad straw hat,
Stood alone in thought intent,
Watching while the other went,
And amid the sunlight red
Paused, with hand held to his head.

In a moment, like a word
Long forgotten until heard,
Like a buried sentiment
Born again to some stray scent,
Like a sound to which the brain
Gives familiar refrain,
Something in the gesture brought
Things forgotten to my thought;

Memory, as I watched the sight.
Flashed from eager light to light.
Remember'd and remember'd not,
Half familiar, half forgot,
Stood the figure, till at last,
Bending eyes on his, I passed,
Gazed again, as loth to go,
Drew the rein, stopt short, and so
Rested, looking back ; when he,
The object of my scrutiny,
Smiled and nodded, saying, "Yes!
Stare your fill, young man !　I guess
You'll know me if we meet again!"

In a moment all my brain
Was illumined at the tone,
All was vivid that had grown
Faint and dim, and straight I knew him,
Holding out my hand unto him,
Smiled, and called him by his name·

M

Wondering, hearing me exclaim,
Abraham Clewson (for 'twas he)
Came more close and gazed at me.
As he gazed, a merry grin
Brighten'd down from eyes to chin :
In a moment he, too, knew me,
Reaching out his hand unto me,
Crying "Track'd, by all that's blue !
Who'd have thought of seeing *you?*"

Then, in double quicker time
Than it takes to make the rhyme,
Abe, with face of welcome bright,
Made me from my steed alight ;
Call'd a boy, and bade him lead
The beast away to bed and feed ;
And, with hand upon my arm,
Led me off into the Farm,
Where, amid a dwelling-place
Fresh and bright as her own face,

With a gleam of shining ware
For a background everywhere,
Free as any summer breeze,
With a bunch of huswife's keys
At her girdle, sweet and mild
Sister Annie blush'd and smiled,—
While two tiny laughing girls,
Peeping at me through their curls,
Hid their sweet shamefacëdness
In the skirts of Annie's dress.

*　　*　　*　　*　　*

That same night the Saint and I
Sat and talked of times gone by,
Smoked our pipes and drank our grog
By the slowly smouldering log,
While the clock's hand slowly crept
To midnight, and the household slept.

" Happy ?" Abe said with a smile,
" Yes, in my *inferior* style,
Meek and humble, not like them
In the New Jerusalem."
Here his hand, as if astray,
For a moment found its way
To his forehead, as he said,
"Reckon they believe I'm dead!
Ah, that life of sanctity
Never was the life for me.
Couldn't stand it wet nor dry,
Hated to see women cry;
Couldn't bear to be the cause
Of tiffs and squalls and endless jaws;
Always felt amid the stir
Jest a whited sepulchre;
And I did the best I could
When I ran away for good.
Yet, for many a night, you know
(Annie, too, would tell you so),

Couldn't sleep a single wink,
Couldn't eat, and couldn't drink,
Being kind of conscience-cleft
For those poor creatures I had left.
Not till I got news from there,
And I found their fate was fair,
Could I set to work, or find
Any comfort in my mind.
Well (here Abe smiled quietly),
Guess they didn't groan for me !
Fanny and Amelia got
Sealed to Brigham on the spot ;
Emmy soon consoled herself
In the arms of Brother Delf ;
And poor Mary one fine day
Packed her traps and tript away
Down to Fresco with Fred Bates,
A young player from the States :
While Sarah, 'twas the wisest plan,
Pick'd herself a single man—

A young joiner fresh come down
Out of Texas to the town—
And he took her with her baby,
And they're doing well as maybe."

Here the Saint with quiet smile,
Sipping at his grog the while,
Paused as if his tale was o'er,
Held his tongue and said no more.
"Good," I said, "but have you done?
You have spoke of all save one—
All your Widows, so bereft,
Are most comfortably left,
But of one alone you said
Nothing.   Is the lady *dead?*"

Then the good man's features broke
Into brightness as I spoke,
And with loud guffaw cried he,
"What, Tabitha? Dead! Not she.

All alone and doing spleudid—
Jest you guess, now, how she's ended !
Give it up ? This very week
I heard she's at Oneida Creek,
All alone and doing hearty,
Down with Brother Noyes's party.
Tried the Shakers first, they say,
Tired of them and went away,
Testing with a deal of bother
This community and t'other,
Till she to Oneida flitted,
And with trouble got admitted.
Bless you, she's a shining lamp,
Tho' I used her like a scamp,
And she's great in exposition
Of the Free Love folk's condition,
Vowing, tho' she found it late,
'Tis the only happy state. . . .

" As for me," added the speaker,
" I'm lower in the scale, and weaker ;

Polygamy's beyond my merits,
Shakerism wears the spirits,
And as for Free Love, why you see
(Here the Saint wink'd wickedly)
With my whim it might have hung
Once, when I was spry and young;
But poor Annie's love alone
Keeps my mind in proper tone,
And tho' my spirit mayn't be strong,
I'm lively—as the day is long."

As he spoke with half a yawn,
Half a smile, I saw the dawn
Creeping faint into the gloom
Of the quickly-chilling room.
On the hearth the wood-log lay,
With one last expiring ray;
Draining off his glass of grog,
Clewson rose and kick'd the log;

As it crumbled into ashes,
Watched the last expiring flashes,
Gave another yawn and said,
" Well! I guess it's time for bed !"

THE END.

PRINTED BY VIRTUS ANO CO., LIMITED, CITY ROAD, LONDON.

ST. ABE AND HIS SEVEN WIVES.

St. Abe and his Seven Wives was written in 1870, at a time when all the Cockney bastions of criticism were swarming with sharp-shooters on the look-out for "the d——d Scotchman" who had dared to denounce Logrolling. It was published anonymously, and simultaneously *The Drama of Kings* appeared with the author's name. The *Drama* was torn to shreds in every newspaper; the Satire, because no one suspected who had written it, was at once hailed as a masterpiece. Even the *Athenæum* cried "all hail" to the illustrious Unknown. The *Pall Mall Gazette* avowed in one breath that Robert Buchanan was utterly devoid of dramatic power, while the author of *St. Abe* was a man of dramatic genius. The secret was well kept, and the bewildered Cocknies did not cease braying their hosannahs even when another anonymous work, *White Rose and Red*, was issued by the same publisher. *St. Abe* went through numerous editions in a very short space of time.

To one familiar with the process of book-reviewing, and aware of the curious futility of even honest literary judgments, there is nothing extraordinary in the facts which I have just stated. Printed cackle about books will always be about as valuable as spoken cackle about them, and the history of literature is one long record of the march of genius through regions of mountainous stupidity. But there were some points about the treatment of *St. Abe* which are worth noting, as illustrating the way in which reviewing "is done" for leading newspapers. Example. The publisher sent out "early sheets" to the great dailies, several of which printed eulogistic reviews. The *Daily Telegraph*, however, was cautious. After receiving the sheets, the acting or sub-editor sent a message round to the publisher saying that a cordial review had been written and was in type, but that "the Chief" wanted to be assured, before committing himself to such an advertisement, about the authorship of the work. "*Is* it by *Lowell?*" queried the jack-in-office; "only inform us in confidence, and the review shall appear." Mr. Strahan either did not reply, or refused to answer the question. Result— the cordial review never appeared at all!

The general impression, however, was that the poem was written by James Russell Lowell. One or two kind critics suggested Bret Harte, but these were in a minority. No one suspected for one moment that the work was written by a Scotchman who, up to that date, had never even visited America. The *Spectator* (A Daniel come to judgment!) devoted a long leading article to proving that humour of this particular kind could have been produced only in the Far West, while a leading magazine bewailed the fact that we had no such humourists in England, since "with Thackeray our last writer of humour left us."

In America itself, the success of the book was less remarkable, and the explanation was given to me in a letter from a publisher in the States, who asserted that public feeling against the Mormons was so fierce and bitter that even a joke at their expense could not be appreciated. "The very subject of Mormondom," wrote my friend, "is regarded as indecent, unsavoury, and offensive." In spite of all, the satire was appreciated, even in America.

Already, however, its subject has ceased to be contemporary and become historical. Mormonism, as I depicted it, is as dead as Slavery, for the Yankee—as I foreshadowed he would do, in this very book—has put down Polygamy. Future generations, therefore, may turn to this book as they will turn to *Uncle Tom's Cabin*, for a record of a system which once flourished, and which, when all is said and done, did quite as much good as harm. I confess, indeed, that I am sorry for the Mormons; for I think that they are more sinned against than sinning. Polygamy is abolished in America, but a far fouler evil, Prostitution, flourishes, in both public and private life. The Mormons crushed this evil and obliterated it altogether, and if they substituted Polygamy, they only did openly and politically what is done, and must be done, clandestinely, in every country, under the present conditions of our civilisation.

The present is the first cheap edition of the book, and the first which bears the author's name on the title page. It will be followed by a cheap edition of *White Rose and Red*. I shall be quite prepared to hear now, on the authority of the newspapers, that the eulogy given to *St. Abe* on its first appearance was all a mistake, and that the writer possesses no humour whatsoever. I was informed, indeed, the other day, by a critic in the *Daily News*, that most of my aberrations proceeded from "a fatal want of humour." The critic was reviewing the *Devil's Case*, and his suggestion was, I presume, that I ought to have perceived the joke of the Nonconformist Conscience and latterday Christianity. I thought that I had done so, but it appears that I had not been funny at all, or not funny enough. But my real misfortune was, that my name was printed on the title page of the work then under review.

I cannot conclude this bibliographical note without a word concerning the remarkable artist who furnished *St. Abe and his Seven Wives* with its original frontispiece. The genius of the late A. B. Houghton is at last receiving some kind of tardy recognition, chiefly through the efforts of Mr. Pennell, whose criticisms on art have done so much to free the air of lingering folly and superstition. When I sought out Mr. Houghton, and persuaded him to put pencil to paper on my behalf, he was in the midst of his life-long struggle against the powers of darkness. He died not long afterwards, prematurely worn out with the hopeless fight. One of the last of the true Bohemians, a man of undoubted genius, he never learned the trick of wearing fine linen and touting for popularity; but those who value good work hold him in grateful remembrance, and I am proud to think that so great a master in black and white honoured me by associating himself with a book of mine.

ROBERT BUCHANAN.

ANTICIPATORY CRITICISMS

ORIGINALLY PREFACED TO

SAINT ABE AND HIS SEVEN WIVES.

———•———

TESTIMONIES OF DISTINGUISHED PERSONS.

I. From P——————t G————t, U.S.

Smart. Polygamy is Greek for Secesh. Guess Brigham will
have to make tracks.

II. From R. W. E———n, Boston, U.S.

Adequate expression is rare. I had fancied the oracles were
dumb, and had returned with a sigh to the enervating society of my
friends in Boston, when your book reached me. To think of it!
In this very epoch, at this very day, poetry has been secreting itself
silently and surely, and suddenly the whole ocean of human thought
is illumined by the accumulated phosphoresence of a subtle and
startling poetic life. . . . Your work is the story of Polygamy
written in colossal cipher for the study of all forthcoming ages.
Triflers will call you a caricaturist, empty solemnities will deem you
a jester. Fools! who miss the pathetic symbolism of Falstaff, and
deem the Rabelaisan epos fit food for mirth. . . . I read it from
first page to last with solemn thoughts too deep for tears. I class
you already with the creators, with Shakespere, Dante, Whitman,
Ellery Channing, and myself.

III. From W——————t W————————n, Washington, U.S.

I Our own feuillage ;
   A leaf from the sweating branches of these States ;
   A fallen symbol, I guess, vegetable, living, human ;
   A heart-beat from the hairy breast of a man.

2 The Salon contents me not;
The fine feathers of New England damsels content me not;
The ways of snobs, the falsettos of the primo tenore, the legs
  of Lydia Thomson's troupe of blondes, content me not;
Nor tea-drinking, nor the twaddle of Mr. Secretary Harlan,
  nor the loafers of the hotel bar, nor Sham, nor Longfellow's Village Blacksmith.

3 But the Prairies content me;
And the Red Indian dragging along his squaw by the scruff of
  the neck;
And the bones of mules and adventurous persons in Bitter
  Creek;
And the oaths of pioneers, and the ways of the unwashed,
  large, undulating, majestic, virile, strong of scent, all
  these content me.

4 Utah contents me;
The City by the margin of the great Salt Lake contents me;
And to have many wives contents me;
Blessed is he who has a hundred wives, and peoples the
  solitudes of these States.

5 Great is Brigham;
Great is polygamy, great is monogamy, great is polyandry,
  great is license, great is right, and great is wrong;
And I say again that wrong is every whit as good as right, and
  not one jot better;
And I say further there is no such thing as wrong, nor any
  such thing as right, and that neither are accountable, and
  both exist only by allowance.

6 O I am wonderful;
And the world, and the sea, and joy and sorrow, and sense
  and nonsense, all content me;
And this book contents me, with its fenillage from the City of
  many wives.

IV. FROM ELDER F——K E——S, OF MT. L———N, U.S.

An amusing attempt to show that polygamy is a social failure.
None can peruse it without perceiving at once that the author
secretly inclines to the ascetic tenets of Shakerism.

V. FROM BROTHER T. H. N———S, O———A C——K.

After perusing this subtle study, who can doubt that Free Love
is the natural human condition? The utter selfishness of the

wretched monogamist-hero repels and sickens us; nor can we look with anything but disgust on the obtusity of the heroine, in whom the author vainly tries to awaken interest. It is quite clear that the reconstruction of Utah on O——a C——k principles would yet save the State from the crash which is impending.

VI. FROM E——A F——NH——M, OF S———N ISLAND.

If *Polygamy* is to continue, then, I say, let *Polyandry* flourish! Woman is the sublimer Being, the subtler Type, the more delicate Mechanism, and, strictly speaking, *needs* many pendants of the inferior or masculine Type to fulfil her mission in perfect comfort. Shall Brigham Young, a mere Man, have sixteen wives; and shall one wretched piece of humanity content *me*, that supreme Fact, *a perfect Woman*, highest and truest of beings under GOD? No; if these things be tolerated, I claim for each Woman, in the name of Light and Law, twenty ministering attendants of the lower race; and the day is near when, if this boon, or any other boon we like to ask, be denied us, it will be *taken with a strong hand!*

VII. FROM T——S C———E, ESQ., CHELSEA, ENGLAND.

The titanic humour of the Conception does not blind me to the radical falseness of the Teaching, wherein, as I shall show you presently, you somewhat resemble the miserable Homunculi of our own literary Wagners; for, if I rightly conceive, you would tacitly and by inference urge that it is expressly part of the Divine Thought that the *Ewigweibliche*, or Woman-Soul, should be *happy*. Now Woman's *mundane* unhappiness, as I construe, comes of her inadequacy; it is the stirring within her of the Infinite against the Finite, a struggle of the spark upward, of the lower to the higher Symbol. Will Woman's Rights Agitators, and Monogamy, and Political Tomfoolery, do what Millinery has failed to do, and waken one Female to the sense of divine Function? It is not *happiness* I solicit for the Woman-Soul, but *Identity;* and the prerogative of Identity is great work, Adequacy, pre-eminent fulfilment of the Function; woman, in this country of rags and shams, being buried quick under masses of Sophistication and Upholstery, oblivious of her divine duty to increase the population and train the young masculine Idea starward. I do not care if the wives of Deseret are pale, or faint, or uncultured, or unhappy; it is enough for me to know that they have a numerous progeny, and believe in Deity or the Divine Essence; and I will not conclude this letter without recording my conviction that yonder man, Brigham Young by name, is perhaps the clearest Intellect now brooding on this planet; that Friedrich was royaller but not greater, and that Bismarck is no more than his equal; and that he, this American, few in words, mark you, but great in deeds, has decided a more stupendous

Question than ever puzzled the strength of either of those others,—the Question of the Sphere and Function in modern life of the ever-agitating FEMININE PRINCIPLE. If, furthermore, as I have ever held, the test of clearness of intellect and greatness of soul be *Success*, at any price and under any circumstances, none but a transcendental Windbag or a pedantic Baccalaureus will doubt my assertion that Young is a stupendous intellectual, ethical, and political Force—a Master-Spirit—a Colossal Being, a moral Architect of sublime cunning—as such to be reverenced by every right-thinking *Man* under the Sun.

VIII. FROM J——N R——N, ESQ., LONDON.

I am not generally appreciated in my own country, because I frequently change my views about religion, art, architecture, poetry, and things in general. Most of my early writings are twaddle, but my present opinions are all valuable. I think this poem, with its nervous Saxon Diction, its subtle humour, its tender pathos and piteousness, the noblest specimen of narrative verse of modern times; and, indeed, I know not where to look, out of the pages of Chaucer, for an equally successful blending of human laughter and ethereal mystery. At the same time, the writer scarcely does justice to the subject on the æsthetic side. A City where the streets are broad and clean and well-watered, the houses surrounded by gardens full of fruit and flowers; where the children, with shining, clean-washed faces, curtsey to the Philosophers in the public places; where there are no brothels and no hells; where life runs fresh, free, and unpolluted,—such a City, I say, can hardly be the symbol of feminine degradation. More than once, tired of publishing my prophetic warnings in the *Daily Telegraph*, I have thought of bending my weary footsteps to the new Jerusalem; and I might have carried out my intention long ago, if I had had a less profound sense of my own unfitness for the duties of a Saint.

IX. FROM M——W A——D, ESQ., ENGLAND.

Your poem possesses a certain rough primitive humour, though it appears to me deficient in the higher graces of *sweetness* and *light*. St. Paul would have entirely objected to the monogamical inference drawn in your epilogue; and the fact that you draw any such inference at all is to me a distressing proof that your tendency is to the Philistinism of those authors who write for the British Matron. I fear you have not read "Merope."

SAINT ABE AND HIS SEVEN WIVES:

A Tale of Salt Lake City.

SOME NOTICES OF THE FIRST EDITION.

From the "GRAPHIC."

"Such vigorous, racy, determined satire has not been met with for many a long day. It is at once fresh and salt as the sea. . . . The humour is exquisite, and as regards literary execution, the work is masterly."

From the "PALL MALL GAZETTE."

"Although in a striking address to Chaucer the author intimates an expectation that Prudery may turn from his pages, and though his theme is certainly a delicate one, there is nothing in the book that a modest man may not read without blinking, and therefore, we suppose, no modest woman. On the other hand, the whole poem is marked with so much natural strength, so much of the inborn faculties of literature—(though they are wielded in a light, easy, trifling way)—that they take possession of our admiration as of right. The chief characteristics of the book are mastery of verse, strong and simple diction, delicate, accurate description of scenery, and that quick and forcible discrimination of character which belongs to men of dramatic genius. This has the look of exaggerated praise. We propose, therefore, to give one or two large samples of the author's quality, leaving our readers to judge from them whether we are not probably right. If they turn to the book and read it through, we do not doubt that they will agree with us."

From the "ILLUSTRATED REVIEW."

"The tale, however, is not to be read from reviews. . . . The variety of interest, the versatility of fancy, the richness of description with which the different lays and cantos are replete, will preclude the possibility of tediousness. To open the book is to read it to the end. It is like some Greek comedy in its shifting scenes, its vivid pictures, its rapidly passing 'dramatis personæ' and supernumeraries. . . . The author of 'St. Abe,' who can write like this, may do more if he will, and even found a new school of realistic and satirical poetry."

From the "DAILY NEWS."

"If the author of a 'Tale of Salt Lake City' be not a new poet, he is certainly a writer of exceedingly clever and effective verses. They have the ring of originality, and they indicate ability to produce something still more remarkable than this very remarkable little piece. It merits a place among works which every one reads with genuine satisfaction. It is a piece which subserves one of the chief ends of poetry, that of telling a tale in an unusually forcible and pleasant way. . . . If it be the author's purpose to furnish a new argument against polygamous Mormons, by showing the ridiculous side of their system, he has perfectly succeeded. The extracts we have given show the varied, fluent, and forcible character of his verse. None who read about Saint Abe and his Seven Wives can fail to be amused and to be gratified alike by the manner of the verse and the matter of the tale."

From the "SCOTSMAN."

"This book does not need much commendation, but it deserves a great deal. The author of 'The Biglow Papers' might have written it, but there are passages which are not unlike Bret Harte; and him we suspect. The authorship, however, may be left out of notice. Men inquire who has written a good book, that they may honour him; but if his name never be heard, the book is none the less prized. In design and construction this work has high merit. It is a good story and it is good poetry. The author is a humourist and a satirist, and he has here displayed all his qualities lavishly."

From the "NONCONFORMIST."

"Amazingly clever. . . . Besides its pure tone deserves warm recognition. The humour is never coarse. There is a high delicacy, which is sufficient to colour and sweeten the whole, as the open spring breeze holds everything in good savour."

From the "SPECTATOR."

"We believe that the new book which has just appeared, 'St. Abe and His Seven Wives,' will paralyze Mormon resistance far more than any amount of speeches in Congress or messages from President Grant, by bringing home to the minds of the millions the ridiculous-diabolic side of the peculiar institution. The canto called 'The Last Epistle of St. Abe to the Polygamists,' with its humorous narrative of the way in which the Saint, sealed to seven wives, fell in love with one, and thenceforward could not abide the jealousy felt by the other six, will do more to weaken the last defence of Mormonism—that after all, the women like it—than a whole ream of narratives about the discontent in Utah. Thousands on whom narrative and argument would make little or no impression, will feel how it must be when many wives with burning hearts watch the husband's growing love for one, when the favourite is sick unto death, and how 'they set their lips and sneered at me and watched the situation,' and will understand that the first price paid for polygamy is the suppression of love, and the second, the slavery of women. The letter in which the first point is proved is too long for quotation, and would be spoiled by extracts; but the second could hardly be better proved than in these humorous lines. . . . The descriptions of Saint Abe and his Seven Wives will be relished by roughs in California as much as by the self-indulgent philosophers of Boston. . . . Pope would have been proud, we fancy, of these terrible lines, uttered by a driver whose *fiancée* has just been beguiled away by a Mormon saint.''

From the "ATHENÆUM."

" ' Saint Abe and his Seven Wives' has a freshness and an originality, altogether wanting in Mr. Longfellow's new work, 'The Divine Tragedy.' In quaint and forcible language—language admirably suited to the theme—the author takes us to the wondrous city of the saints, and describes its inhabitants in a series of graphic sketches. The hero of the story is Saint Abe, or Abraham Clewson, and in giving us his history the author has really given us the inner life of the Mormon settlement. In his pages we see the origin of the movement, the reasons why it has increased, the internal weakness of the system, and the effect it produces on its adherents. We are introduced to the saints, whom we see among their pastures, in their homes, in their promenades, and in their synagogue.''

From the "FREEMAN."

" A remarkable poem. . . . The production is anonymous, but whoever the author may be there can be no question that he is a poet, and one of vast and varied powers. The inner life of Mormondom is portrayed with a caustic humour equal to anything in ' The Biglow Papers '; and were it not for the exquisite elegance of the verse we should think that some parts of the poem were written by Robert Browning. The hero of the poem is a Mormon, who fares so badly as a polygamist that he elopes with one of his seven wives—the one whom he really loves; and the story is a most effective exposure of the evils which necessarily attach to polygamy.''

From the WEEKLY REVIEW."

" There can be no doubt that it is worthy of the author of ' The Biglow Papers.' Since that work was published, we have received many humorous volumes from across the Atlantic, but nothing equal to ' St. Abe.' As to its form, it shows that Mr. Lowell has been making advances in the poetic art; and the substance of it is as strong as anything in the entire range of English satirical literature.''

From the "BRITISH QUARTERLY REVIEW."

"The writer has an easy mastery over various kinds of metre, and a felicity of easy rhyming which is not unworthy of our best writers of satire. . . . The prevailing impression of the whole is of that easy strength which does what it likes with language and rhythm. . . . . The style is light and playful, with admirable touches of fine discrimination and rich humour; but the purpose is earnest. . . . . The book is a very clever and a very wholesome one. It is one of those strong, crushing, dramatic satires, which do more execution than a thousand arguments."

From "TEMPLE BAR."

"It is said to be by Lowell. Truly, if America has more than one writer who can write in such a rich vein of satire, humour, pathos, and wit, as we have here, England must look to her laurels. . . . This is poetry of a high order. Would that in England we had humourists who could write as well. But with Thackeray our last writer of humour left us."

From the "WESTMINSTER REVIEW."

"'Saint Abe and his Seven Wives' may lay claim to many rare qualities. The author possesses simplicity and directness. To this he adds genuine humour and intense dramatic power. Lastly, he has contrived to give a local flavour, something of the salt of the Salt Lake to his characters, which enables us to thoroughly realise them. . . . We will not spoil the admirable canto 'Within the Synagogue' by any quotation, which, however long, cannot possibly do it justice. We will merely say that this one bit is worth the price of the whole book. In the author we recognise a true poet, with an entirely original vein of humour."

From the "MANCHESTER GUARDIAN."

"It is thoroughly American, now rising into a true imaginative intensity, but oftener falling into a satirical vein, dealing plainly enough with the plague-spots of Salt Lake society and its wily, false prophets. . . . Like most men capable of humour, the author has command of a sweeter and more harmonious manner. Indeed, the beautiful descriptive and lyrical fragments stand in vivid and refreshing relief to the homely staple of the poem."

From the "TORONTO GLOBE."

"It is impossible to deny that the praises bestowed on 'St. Abe and his Seven Wives' as a work of literary power are deserved."